Indiony.

The Tingle

Audrey,

Thanks for buying
a copy, I hope you
like it,

— Frankie
Sepulveda

To order additional copies, please contact us.
BookSurge, LLC
www.booksurge.com
1-866-308-6235
orders@booksurge.com

FRANKIE
W. SYMONDS

THE
TINGLE

ABOUT AN AMERICAN BOY

Name of Publisher
2003

The Tingle

I would like to dedicate this to my grandmother, Pat. You helped me become a nice person. You also gave me my raunchy sense of humor. I love and miss you.

I would also like to thank my cousin, Jimmy, who went to Mexico with me. Don't worry. Melvin is not based on you!

CHAPTER 1

This is ridiculous!" Brian McMahon stated to his mother, as they drove.

"Calm down, honey. This will be good for you. You're depressed and it can't go on. You have to be happy or else I can't be happy."

"Oh come on, Edna. You're far too optimistic. I've grown used to my unhappiness and I honestly believe nothing can be done about it."

"Honey, why do you insist on calling me by my first name?" Edna asked. It bothered her a great deal that her son always called her by her first name, but he had been doing it since he was a child.

"I call you Edna because Edna is your name."

"But normal kids don't call their mothers by their first name."

"Well I'm sorry. I guess you'll have to deal with it."

Their destination was the psychiatrists office. Edna had called and made an appointment for her son earlier in the week. You see, for quite some time now, Brian had been showing visible signs of depression. Seeing the McMahon family is known for their constant happiness, Edna has no choice but to do something about her son. His unhappiness made no sense to her, especially because she raised him with as much love as she could come up with.

"Here we are, honey," Edna said, with a warm smile on her

face. She caressed her son's head. "Everything's going to be fine. There's no need to worry."

Brian pushed her hand away.

"It won't be fine, Edna. I'm only doing this to appease to you."

"As long as you're doing it."

They got out of the car and began to walk. Seeing that finding parking in Boston is nearly impossible, they had quite a way to walk, having had to park far from the office. As they walked they came across everything that one might see when walking down the streets of Boston. Brian scrutinized every homeless person and every hand- holding couple that they crossed paths with, giving both equal looks of disgust.

"Brian! Don't give people dirty looks, honey. Come on!" Edna said, grabbing him by the hand.

"I am seventeen years old! I don't need or want you holding my hand."

After walking for at least fifteen minutes, they finally came to the office.

"We're here, honey."

"I don't want to."

"You said that you wanted to appease to me."

"I changed my mind."

"You can't change your mind," Edna said, grabbing his hand and pulling him through the door.

When they entered the waiting room, Brian looked around. "I don't like the smell," he said, cringing. In response, Edna simply frowned at him.

"Sit down. I'll go tell them we're here."

"Fine."

Brian went over to the chairs in the waiting room and sat in one. As soon as he sat, a female, about his age, came out from the doctor's office and sat in the chair next to him. She looked at him and smiled. He looked her in the eye, then moved over to the next chair. The look on her face made her seem as if she was offended, but he didn't care.

"All set," Edna said, sitting down in the chair that Brian had just gotten up from. "The doctor will be seeing us any minute."

"Great," Brian said, with a hint of sarcasm in his voice.

Within a matter of minutes, the person behind the desk told Brian that the doctor would now see him. He went to the back and walked through the door of the doctor's office, closed the door, looked at the doctor, and turned red. The individual before him was an immensely obese woman sitting in a large chair. He tried his hardest not to laugh.

"Have a seat," said the obese woman.

Brian sat.

"So, You're Brian McMahon," she said, looking at papers on a clipboard she was holding.

"Yes, yes I am."

"So what brings you here today?"

"My mother."

"Don't be silly. I mean what problem do you have that would make you feel the need to seek my help?"

"I don't know. I honestly don't think that seeking your help was necessary. But the problem that made my mother bring me here, well, I've been unhappy for quite some time."

"You've been unhappy? Why is that?"

"I can't do this!" Brian said, standing up. "I don't want to tell you any of this stuff. It's none of your business."

"Sit back down," she said, squirming in her chair. "I'm sorry. I didn't do this right. Just sit down. I promise something good will come of this."

He sat.

"My name is Dr. Hubbard."

"Well, that's good. You already have my name in your papers. So now that we're acquainted and all, just make this as quick as you can, Dr. Hubbard."

"I'm trying. Now you have to tell me exactly what it is that's been troubling you."

"You won't repeat any of this, will you?"

"Don't worry. I can't repeat any of this."

"Alright. Fine," Brian said. He let out a long sigh and began. "Well you see, I am a seventeen year old junior in high school. I get straight A's. I'm the president of the student council. I'm the captain of the football team. And not to toot my horn, but every girl at my school loves me."

"So what's the problem?" Hubbard asked, giving him a unique look.

"I'm alone! That's the problem. I can't find the right girl."

"But you said_"

"Don't say it! Just because all the girls I know want me does not mean I want all or any of them."

"Well you must like some of them."

"I don't."

This was a big shock to Dr. Hubbard. Brian was a very good looking young man. She even had a hard time listening to him speak without staring. She had never seen or heard of a case that even resembled this. Any teenage boy would take advantage of bunches of girls at their leisure.

"Well, why don't you like any of them?" asked Hubbard.

"There are different reasons. There's always something that just isn't right. Some people just get on my nerves. But, to be fully honest, I find just about everyone extremely ugly.

I walk down the street and see two people, happily walking together, giving off the impression that they are madly in love. I do not even comprehend how they do this! They are always so awkward looking!"

Dr. Hubbard opened her mouth in disbelief. She was certain that her ears were deceiving her and she was even more certain that Brian was just a bad human being. Still, she was getting paid and she had to make an attempt to help.

"Well, are there any girls you find attractive at all?"

"I find some people more attractive than others, but none enough to really consider."

"Why don't you ever go out with the people you find most attractive?"

"It will just turn out bad," Brian said, running his fingers through his naturally golden- blonde locks of hair.

"How do you know it will turn out bad? If you've never had anything to do with these girls, how can you be sure of how things will work out?"

"Listen. If I get such strong negative feelings about something, it just doesn't seem likely that it will work out for the best."

"Sometimes following your own feelings isn't the best thing to do."

"That truly is something that someone like you would say."

"Someone like me?"

"A psychiatrist," he said, with an intentionally mean smirk on his face.

"Fine. Be harsh. I am just trying to help you," Hubbard said, rubbing her fat stomach. "I get the impression that you listen to yourself on a pretty frequent basis."

"That's correct."

"Well, you're the depressed one sitting in a psychiatrist's office, aren't you?"

"That was harsh. But, I guess you have a point."

"Yes I do have a point," she said proudly. "After all, I am the professional. So, your best bet is to listen to what I have to say."

"Alright. What is it that you have to say?"

"I say that you agree to go out with the next girl who asks."

"But_"

"No but's! Listen, you can't expect the girl of your dreams to just casually walk into your life and turn your world upside down. It just doesn't happen that way, no matter how good looking you are. If you want to be happy you have to be a little lenient," Hubbard said, caressing her double chin.

Brian couldn't help but ask himself how the doctor knew all of this. After all, she was an exceptionally unattractive woman who seemed to be as much of a stranger to love as he was, for different reasons of course. Also, he was very angry. Even if she was right, he didn't want to do something he was so strictly against.

"Fine." Brian said quietly.

"What's that?"

"I said fine,"

"Good. We're making great progress already. I think we've accomplished as much as we possibly can today. Now, I want you to go out to the front, make an appointment for next week, then tell you're parents about what we've decided."

"Okay then."

Brian left the office, made his appointment, and told Edna, with hesitance of course, what had happened. Edna then

6

took Brian out to dinner to celebrate, being the perky and optimistic woman that she was.

CHAPTER 2

It was now Monday, two days after Brian's appointment with Dr. Hubbard. Brian was sitting on a toilet in a bathroom stall, as he often did, to keep away from the females. He was deeply pondering whether to come out of the bathroom and into the public, allowing the girls a chance to ask him out. He didn't want to do this at all. He knew, however, that if he didn't, he would have Edna pestering him constantly about it. Also, he knew that he had another appointment with Dr. Hubbard that coming Saturday, and that she would also pester him if he didn't follow her advice.

Though Brian was totally against going out with any of the girls at his school, he had to admit that the words of Hubbard had affected him. He knew that there was something wrong with his overall mood. He was never happy and this scared him. Now that Hubbard pointed out that dodging females will do nothing but keep him in his state of unhappiness, he felt different; more scared. This fear is what made him decide to come out of the bathroom.

He took a swift turn to the left as soon as he exited the bathroom. He was heading toward his locker, looking in every direction for admirers to dodge. The coast seemed to be clear. His locker was now right down the hall. He picked up his speed. He was sure that this was going to be the first time he had made it to his locker without a member of the female gender going nuts over him. He smiled, as he walked the last few steps to his locker, knowing that if he didn't have any girls around him, he couldn't possibly turn any down. Therefore, he wasn't going back on his word at all.

He stood in front of his locker and let out a sigh of relicf. He began fidgeting with the lock, undoing the combination, smiling as he did so. Just then, he felt, and heard breathing on his neck.

"Brian," said a voice from behind him.

Brian quickly turned around. "What?" It was Edna Hutchinson who spoke his name. "Hello Edna. Can I help you?"

"You definitely can help me. I was wondering if you'd like to maybe go the movies with me Friday night?"

Brian gave her a look. Edna was by no means a bad looking girl, nor was she a girl with a bad personality. There was, however, one thing about her that Brian couldn't possibly deal with.

"I- I. I'm sorry no. Just no. Well, you see," Brian said, speaking very fast, "it just won't work. Nothing will work. You share my mom's name and I just don't really care for her. Your name is just a bad sign and well, no."

Brian slammed his locker shut and quickly walked away, not looking back at poor, crushed Edna.

"Why the hell did it have to be her, of all people. That wasn't very fair," he said as he walked.

The bell for first period rang, and Brian walked quickly to room 56 for his American History class. He plopped himself down in the same seat every day. Shortly after he sat down, another boy came into the classroom and sat down next to him. Brian smiled at the boy who sat next to him, for it was one of the few people he actually cared for.

"Melvin! My dear friend. How are you?" Brian asked.

"Eh. Same old stuff. You know."

Melvin McMahon was Brian's cousin on the father's side. Melvin was the opposite of Brian in every definition of the word. He wore thick glasses. They did not, however, take away from his handsomeness, seeing he did not have any. He had red hair, in which he put a lot of gel to make it look halfway presentable, as opposed to Brian's beautiful golden locks of hair, which naturally fell in an attractive way. Melvin was covered from head to toe in orangish freckles.

Brian liked Melvin because he was a pretty nice person and Brian believed he was one of the few people who actually understood him. Brian felt bad for him. Melvin was an angry young man. He was jealous of all who had it better than him, which were most of the people he knew. He was a nerd who was constantly harassed and picked on. He had lived in Brian's shadow for his whole life. He had accepted it, though, and he and Brian were very close.

Both Brian and his cousin shared a longing desire to have something romantic happen between them and a female. They both desired it for different reasons. While Brian was a hopeless romantic who wanted nothing but a meaningful, lifelong relationship with the girl of his dreams, Melvin wanted nothing more than kinkiness and blowjobs. Both of them felt that they were having no luck and though neither of them could understand the other's reasons for wanting a girl, their unhappiness seemed to bring the both of them together.

"I'm sure something will change for us soon enough," Brian said quietly. The class had already started and he was trying to make it so the teacher wouldn't hear him.

"Really?"

"No. I'm just trying to be nice. We're both screwed. I get no love and you get no action."

"I could kill you sometimes. You could get any girl at this school to go down on you and you don't."

"Having girls go down on you means nothing. Once it's over, it's over. In the end you gain nothing from it at all." Brian rolled his eyes as he made the statement.

"You're a friggen nut. And you do gain something from it. You gain..."

"Shut up both you McMahon boys," the teacher said.

"I'll finish later."

***

Lunch was after fourth period. Brian and Melvin sat together, as they always did, and discussed things, things that were important to them.

"Brian," Melvin said, sitting down. "As I was saying. You do gain something from having a girl go down on you. You gain your manhood."

"I don't care about my manhood. The way I feel, I wouldn't be much less happy prancing around in a hot pink evening gown."

Melvin looked at him with a confused expression.

"It get's worse, though, Melvin. Now I have problems being added to my problems. You see, a few days ago I had some shrink appointment. Edna says I'm depressed. Yes, I will admit I'm at my lowest level of happiness ever, but depressed? That may be going overboard."

"Uh- huh"

"Well, anyways. The doctor, this really fat thing, she gave me a huge lecture and it scared the living daylights out of me."

"How did she do that?"

"It made me think. She made it clear to me that I'll never be happy if I keep on turning every girl down."

"At least you have girls to turn down!" Melvin exclaimed.

"Stop it, Melvin. You can bitch all you want when I'm done. This is really important."

Melvin gave Brian the middle finger. Brian ignored it.

"So, you see. The fat doctor and I made a deal that I'd say yes to the first girl who asks me out. I already blew it though. Edna Hutchinson asked me to do something with her."

"Edna's really hot."

"Edna's name is Edna. It just wouldn't work."

"You're a sick kid."

"Maybe. But what does that matter."

"If I were you, I'd fuck all those easy girls and I'd be a happy person. You could be a happy person if you would just let yourself be a happy person."

"Hmm. You're a sex- obsessed freak. I think you're the sick kid."

"We're both sick in our own special way, I'm sure," Melvin said, with a twisted smile on his face that only Brian wouldn't be afraid of.

The cafeteria lights that were shining on the faces of Brian and Melvin were blocked. They were in the presence of a shadow. They both looked up to see what it was.

"Rebecca!" Melvin said happily. "How are you today?"

"Uh, yea. I'm fine."

Other than the few exchanged words, she ignored Melvin.

"Brian, what are you doing Friday night?"

Brian and Melvin made eye contact. Brian smirked. Melvin sneered.

"Nothing," Brian said casually.

"Nothing, hmm," Rebecca said, trying her very best to sound sexy. "Well, would you like to do something?"

"Something as in what?"

"Something as in with me!" She said, being perky.

"No, no, no. You don't understand. I didn't ask who I would be doing this something with. I asked what the something I would be doing was."

"Uh, well. Umm."

"What I'm asking is what are we going to be doing!?" Brian said loudly, slamming his fist on the table.

Brian had a very hard time tolerating people that he didn't find very interesting. He did not find Rebecca very interesting at all.

She grew uncomfortable and quiet as a result of Brian's yelling. After a few seconds to recover, she ignored his fit. She had to ignore it, seeing he was the best looking boy in her school and she, a shallow young lady.

"Well, we could go to the movies or something, couldn't we?"

"Yes. We could. In fact, let's. Let's go to the movies Friday night. Seven?"

"Yes! Yes seven is fine, so very fine. Couldn't even be finer!"

"Seven it is then."

"Yes!" Rebecca yelled as she stood up.

Rebecca then skipped away in the most joyous manner possible, still not able to believe that what had just happened did actually happen.

Melvin looked at Brian. "You lucky piece of shit," he said, not sarcastically.

The bell rang for fifth period and lunch was over.

***

Seeing Brian and Melvin lived close to one another, they

walked home with each other every day. Today was no different than any other day.

"Thank God you said yes. If you didn't I would have had to kill you," said Melvin.

"It's hardly worth killing anyone over."

"Rebecca is the hottest girl in the whole school! The hottest girl is always worth killing someone over."

"She's flawed."

"Everyone's flawed. Get used to it."

"No. I mean yes, everyone is flawed all in all. But there's more to it than that," Brian started. Melvin was pretty sure that a fairly long speech was about to be given by Brian. "You see, yes, everyone is flawed. But there is someone, maybe even a few someones, for everyone. These are the people whose flaws you can completely overlook. These are the people that you were made for. It's called compatibility."

Brian looked at Melvin and managed to crack a very small smile.

"Compatibility and perfection are two completely different things."

"That's funny. I see no difference."

CHAPTER 3

It was Thursday night of that same week. Brian was sitting on the back porch of his house alone. He spent a lot of his time there. It was a good thinking spot, and thinking was one of his most practiced hobbies. It was a typical April night. It was getting warm after the cold Boston winter. The aroma of newly budding flowers filled the air. Nature was doused with color for the first time in many months. This was the time of year when everyone seemed to get struck by the dreaded "spring fever". And even Brian was experiencing it. He was in an unusually good mood this night, as he sat on his porch. This night was a special night, not only because of the weather, but because of the thoughts that were coming into Brian's head. Brian was a deep thinker, but tonight, the depth of his thoughts seemed to reach a whole new level.

Brian thought: It must be just me. It must be something internal. There's no way it's external and there's no way this is common. If it was, everyone would be the way I am. And if I'm so unhappy, why is everyone so jealous of me? Why does Melvin consider me lucky? I don't consider myself lucky at all. But maybe, seeing everyone seems to think I'm in a great position, I actually am. Maybe It's just me. Maybe.

This was the first time Brian had ever even put into consideration that maybe he might actually be in a good position when it came to him and the female sex. More important than that, it was the first time that he had ever put into consideration that it might be just him, that he might have an unusual problem, that he might even be looking for something that doesn't exist.

Edna came out onto the porch and sat in a chair directly next to Brian. She was silent for the first few moments she was there, only staring at Brian. He was somewhere else. He was looking off into the distance, indulged in his own mind.

"Honey?" Edna said.

He continued to look at the nothing he was looking at.

"Brian. Brian! Snap out of it, sweetheart. Dinner's ready."

He stepped back into reality.

"Dinner? What's for dinner?"

"Pork chops, honey. Your favorite."

"My favorite?"

"Uh, sure," Edna said hesitatingly.

Both Brian and Edna went back into the house together. They went into the kitchen. Sitting at the table was Harry, Brian's father. He had a smile on his face, with a perkiness which was the equivalent to the perkiness Edna was most known for.

Harry McMahon and Edna were soul mates without a doubt. Every aspect of Harry seemed to compliment Edna and every aspect of Edna seemed to compliment Harry. They never fought and they looked good together. They were a good looking couple. And they fit the stereotype of a good looking couple quite well, excessively perky and upbeat, always a mortal enemy to anything that attempted to bring them down.

"Brian! My favorite son," said Harry.

"I'm you're only son."

"Well that just makes the statement more true, doesn't it?" Harry said with a smile on his face that could be easily compared to that of a man in a toothpaste commercial. "How was your day?"

"Fine."

Brian cringed when the said this. When he day was brought up, it only made him recall the swarms of females that were buzzing all day. You see, Rebecca was very proud of the fact that she and Brian were going on a date the next night. Obviously, she made this known to all the girls who weren't her. This only drove them even harder to pester Brian.

"So tomorrow's the big night, right?" Edna asked with a twinkle in her eye.

"What big night might that be?"

"Your date with that girl, silly."

"I hardly consider that big," Brian said, being very cool about it.

The fact of the matter, however, was that Brian really did care. It wasn't that he was looking forward to the date, because he wasn't. But it had been on his mind a lot. He was petrified. She was a girl and he was going out with her on a date. He knew that the whole meaning of a date with a female was to get to know them better than you did before the date. He didn't want to know Rebecca any better than he did. He was scared of what would happen if he got to know her, or any girl for that matter, any better than he already did.

Edna placed the pot roast in the middle of the table. She made this pot roast with a great deal of care. She put a great deal of care into most of the things she did, especially things that had to do with her family. To Edna, nothing was more important than having a good family; a family to be proud of.

Brian, it is very big. It's your first date. Now I know it's a little odd for such a good looking kid to have his first date at your age, but it doesn't matter. Everyone's first date is always important."

"Edna, no. You have to understand that I'm only following the doctors orders. Just like someone takes a prescription pill, I'm taking this prescription date."

This was all a lie. Brian wasn't "only following the doctors orders" like he claimed. Brian was doing this for a change, a much needed change. It was no longer him not wanting to do something. He had spent far too much time worrying about what he didn't want. It was now time to focus on what he did want. He didn't want Rebecca, but she was practice, as mean as that may be.

"Oh come on! You must be a little excited," Edna said, lightly putting her fist down on the table. "I'm sure she's a very nice girl."

"Pretty too," Harry added. "You're both wrong. I'm not excited. And in the personality department, well, she's quite typical. She's not mean, but I'd hardly consider her nice. And looks. Her hair is sort of mousy, not a particular preference of mine."

Edna and Harry both gave Brian a puzzled look. Harry broke the silence.

"I'm sure she's better than that, Brian. Sometimes you can make things sound so much worse than they actually are."

"You know, I can bet you you're wrong, Brian!" said Edna.

"I'm not wrong. I am not excited. She's not even worth excitement."

Edna stood up.

"Edna. Edna! What the hell are you doing?"

"Proving you wrong, honey."

She walked to the phone, picked it up, and began to dial. Brian stood immediately.

"Who are you calling?!"

Edna put her finger up in an attempt to silence Brian.

"Edna! God damn it, Edna. What the hell are you doing?"

"Melvin? Hi Melvin, how are you?" Edna said into the phone. "Yea that's good to hear. Me too. Well, you see, I made a pot roast and there's plenty to go around. I wouldn't want it to go to waste and it's always a joy to have my favorite nephew over for dinner. What? You will? Great. I'll see you in a few."

Edna hung up the phone, smirking at Brian as she did so. She then strutted, not walked, back to her chair and sat.

Harry and his brother had decided to buy houses that were right next to each other. Melvin lived right next door and would be there any second, which was good for Edna and bad for Brian.

Any second arrived and the doorbell rang.

"Good, Brian. He's here."

Edna went to the door, strutting like she had done before. She answered it with her usual smile that Brian hated.

"Melvin! Great to see you. Come in and sit down," Edna said, wrapping her arms around her nephew.

"Is that Melvin? It is. Get over here and give your old uncle a hand shake!" exclaimed Harry.

After Melvin had met the requests of his aunt and uncle, he joined everyone at the dinner table. Brian said nothing to him. Trying to warn Melvin of what was to come, he gave him a stern look.

Edna gave Melvin a few minutes to eat, so that he wouldn't be too suspicious about the interrogation. Once she had deemed him good and comfortable, she went in for the kill.

"So, Melvin."

"Yea, Auntie Edna?"

"That girl Brian has a date with tomorrow night, is she nice?"

"Yes. I'd say that she's pretty nice."

"Is she a looker?" asked Harry.

"A what- er?"

"Is she good looking?"

"Oh yea. She's really hot, uh, pretty. Yes, she's really pretty."

"Hmm," said Edna. "That's funny. Brian made her sound like she was awful or something."

"She's far from awful."

Brian was angry.

"Alright! Are we done with this discussion now. Can't you understand, Edna, that some people have different tastes than other people. Just because Melvin likes her doesn't mean that I have to."

"But Brian, you don't like anyone."

Brian hated being questioned by his mother. Even more, he hated when his mother made true statements about him that he didn't want to hear. She was completely right by saying that he liked no one. He wasn't proud of this.

"Well, I'm done," Brian said. "Come one, Melvin. I say we take a nice walk. I need some fresh air and I'm sure after sitting at the dinner table with these wretched heathens, you do too."

"Uh, if you want me..."

"I do. Let's go."

Melvin said goodbye to his aunt and uncle. Brian said goodbye to no one. They both left for their walk.

"Melvin! Couldn't you have just lied for me?"

"I didn't know you wanted me to."

"What the hell did you think the look I gave you was for?"

"Well, you're not exactly the most happy person on Earth. It's not unusual for you to give people dirty looks for no reason at all."

"Thank you," Brian said with sarcasm.

All the conversations that took place this night made Brian realize more than he ever had before that he was not necessarily a good person. A desire to change existed deep in the pit of his stomach.

"Where are we going?"

"I don't know. Maybe we can go to the playground. It's pretty late. I'm sure all the little kids are gone for the night."

"Sounds fine to me."

It was getting dark. The sun was beginning to set over the trees in the park where Brian and Melvin sat. They had made themselves comfortable on the now abandoned swing set.

"I'm scared, Melvin."

"Of what?"

"Everything."

"You can't be scared of everything."

"Hmm," said Brian, pondering his next statement. "Well I'm scared of a lot of things."

"Tomorrow night?"

"Yea, but not just that. That's really the least of my worries. You see, I'm finally going on a date with a girl. Apparently, this girl is God's gift to men. I don't see it! And if I don't see it in her, God's gift to men, well, Am I ever going to see it in anyone?"

"Don't get so worked up. I'm sure you'll find someone."

"Why?"

"I don't know. It just seems like you will."

"People are naturally optimistic when it has to do with other people's lives. You don't mean what you say. I won't believe it til things change."

"Stop bitching, Brian. I'm not happy either. I'm getting less than you and I stay pretty quiet."

"You choose to stay quiet. And you're the only one I complain to."

This was their mutual relationship at its height thus far. Brian was Melvin's only form of sanity while Melvin was Brian's only form of sanity. They were both unhappy people. Watching each other be unhappy made the both of them feel better about themselves. In a way, they needed each other.

"Brian, not to change the subject, but look at the sun."

Brian looked up at the trees, where a pinkish- orange, gleaming light hovered.

"It's kind of pretty."

"It is. Maybe it's a sign."

"It's pretty, yes. But don't be stupid. It's just the sun setting."

"Maybe."

CHAPTER 4

It was three o' clock. Brian had just walked in to his house from school. He went directly into his bedroom, set his bag down, and sat on his bed. He got up, looked in his mirror, ran his hands through his hair, raised an eyebrow, and sat back down. The date was in four hours.

Meanwhile, Rebecca was at home, moving as fast as her body could carry her. She was plotting her outfit for the date with great thought. For her, great thought was hard thing to achieve. For this occasion, however, it was achievable. Within ten minutes of coming home, she had already called five people. She made it a point to each of them that she was going out with Brian McMahon and they weren't. There were many more people on her list to make similar phone calls to.

Brian still sat on his bed.

She turned on the shower. She gathered every scented item she owned into the bathroom for later use. She stepped into the shower and stayed in there for an hour, making sure to rid her body of any impurity that might turn Brian off.

Brian still sat on his bed.

She stepped out of the shower and dried her body thoroughly with her softest towel. She put on a scented deodorant and rubbed her whole body down with scented lotion. She looked down at her naked body and smiled, admiring the Brazilian wax job she had gotten the day before.

Brian now lay on his bed.

She pulled her black thong up tightly between her legs. She put on a black padded bra with the intentions of making her already large breasts look larger than they were. She put on her tight pink tank top, pulled her black skirt up, and slipped on black shoes.

Brian stayed laying on his bed.

She sprayed her hair, making it look as sexy as the hair of a seventeen year old girl could possibly look. Finally, she made her face up. She was ready.

Brian got up, went into the bathroom, took a piss, and brushed his teeth. He was ready.

***

"Brian, make me proud. I'm begging you, don't screw this up. You don't know how big this is," said Melvin into the phone.

"I'm going to try to make this as good as I can. I don't know how well it's going to work, but you know that I'll try."

"No I don't."

"Come on, Melvin, have a little faith in me."

"You've never given me a good reason to."

"Well, hopefully that'll change after tonight. But I still don't even know why I'm so nervous about tonight. I'm not attracted to her."

"I think you're just trying to prove to everyone that you can actually interact with a girl like a normal person."

"I think I'm trying to prove it to myself."

"Yea well, I don't know," said Melvin, beginning to feel jealous of the fact that Brian was going out with Jessica and not him. And Brian didn't even want her. Why would God put Melvin through this? Ah! "Well yea, Brian. Good luck! Bye." Melvin hung up the phone without a goodbye from Brian. The fit of anger was sudden. Melvin lit one of his mom's cigarettes and watched T. V. to calm himself down.

Brian left the house to meet Rebecca.

***

Brian found a seat in the crowded train. He did he best to ignore the smelly foreign woman who was sitting next to him. The ugly couple across from him, however, was a hard thing to ignore. He found himself staring at them and giving them looks as if he was plotting their murder. They saw the looks and decided to ignore them, assuming he was just another oddball prancing around in the downtown Boston area.

Though the looks Brian gave them were because of the fact that he was jealous of their happiness, his jealousy wasn't the biggest issue. He couldn't help but ask himself, just as he asked himself so very often, how two extremely unattractive people could be happy together. He stared, and stared, and stared. They were holding hands, and smiling. They were both overweight. It drove Brian nuts and confused him greatly.

The train pulled up at his stop. He stood up and began walking to the door. He made a brief stop on his journey from his seat to the door. He stood in front of the seated, happy, ugly couple and looked down at them. The male half of the couple looked up.

"Yes?"

Brian turned red. "I don't fucking get you people!" he yelled. He then stormed off the train.

Rebecca was standing in front of the theater. She had been waiting there for some time. She had to be there early, incase Brian had also decided to arrive early. Of course, he didn't. He was on time.

He noticed her standing at the front door before she

was even aware of his presence. He noticed that she was all dolled up for him. He felt almost bad for not putting an equal amount of effort into getting ready for her. Sadly, almost bad was as bad as he was going to allow himself to feel.

He began to approach her. She saw him coming.

"Brian! Brian! Hey, I'm over here!"

"I'm five feet away. There's no need to yell," said Brian.

"Oh, well, I'm real sorry. So well, can we go in?"

"We can."

They entered the main lobby of the theater and both looked up at the movies and times simultaneously .

"What are we going to see?" Brian asked.

"I don't know. It's completely up to you."

"I honestly don't care."

"Oh," Rebecca said quietly. "Well, just pick something random," she said, regaining her upbeat tone.

Brian was astounded by the fact that she knew what the word random meant. He was tempted to put her on the spot and ask her to define it for him, but he didn't want to embarrass her.

"Fine, something random."

Brian walked up to the man behind the counter and asked for two tickets to some movie he had never heard of, hoping that the theater wouldn't be crowded. He hated crowds.

The man handed Brian the two tickets and he realized something. He had just spent a whole ten dollars on Rebecca. This sickened him. He knew it was customary to buy the girl's ticket.

Is she really worth going out with if spending ten dollars on her makes me sick? Brian asked himself silently.

Thoughts of Edna and Hubbard harassing him came into

his mind, making him far more sick than the purchasing of the tickets had.

"Alright, lets go," he said to Rebecca with a forced jolliness.

Brian and Rebecca entered the theater. Brian looked up and saw that there weren't very many people seeing the movie, just as he had hoped for.

"Let's sit in the back," Rebecca said.

"Why the back?"

"The back is nice and dark and more private. You can see the movie better from the back."

Brian was aware of her intentions, but something inside him told him to give in, and he did.

"Fine, we can sit in the back."

The movie hadn't even started when Rebecca placed her hand in between Brian's legs.

"No!" Brian said, pushing her hand away.

"What's wrong?"

"This is a public place. You can't do that here."

"I've done it before," Rebecca said, dumbly.

"I can only imagine the kinds of guys who were on the receiving end of those sorts of actions."

Brian regretted letting Rebecca talk him into sitting in the back. In those few moments, he decided to never let something inside him tell him what to do again.

"Well can we at least make out?" Rebecca asked, seeming antsy.

"Not now. I just want to watch the movie. Isn't that what people are supposed to do when they go to the movies?"

"Not always."

"Always in my case!" he snapped.

"Sorry."

Despite the fact that she apologized to him, Rebecca tried again and again to put the moves on him and again and again he refused to let it happen. He longed for the movie to end.

The ninety minutes of crotch grabbing and attempted tongue action finally came to a halt. Brian was thrilled to get out of the theater, but he wasn't completely free. There was still the trip home. He knew it was customary to escort his date back to her place of residence. Brian had nothing better to do with his time and being customary seemed like a good way to use the time that would be wasted anyways.

"So, you liked the movie?" asked Brian as he and Rebecca walked toward the train station.

"Oh yea, of course. It was especially good because I got to go with you."

Corny. Brian said on the inside.

"I see. Well, yes, um, I don't know."

Brian approached the window and purchased one token for himself. He put the token in the slot and entered before Rebecca had finished buying hers. He had already spent, or blown, in his eyes, ten dollars on Rebecca that night. That was enough. She could pay for her own token.

"Brian! Wait for me!" Rebecca yelled loudly, too loudly for Brian's liking.

"Yea!"

A train pulled up as soon as they reached the bottom of the stairs. They got on. Brian found a lone empty seat and sat in it, leaving Rebecca to stand. She didn't even consider complaining.

Brian began inspecting people around him, as he always did when he was in public. It seemed, by complete coincidence, that the couple who sat across from him on his earlier train ride was now seated directly across from him again. He stared, this time, more than he had the previous time.

"Isn't that the weird kid who yelled some random shit at us earlier?" the male half of the couple asked his female partner.

"You're right, it is," said the female half.

As if he was in a trance, Brian stood up from his seat, still keeping his eyes on the unattractive couple. He approached them slowly, with a look on his face that signified nothing but complete mortification.

"You again," said the male half. "What do you want now?"

"Are you, in love?" Brian asked hesitatingly.

"Yes, we are in love. I'd say we're in love. Wouldn't you, honey?"

"Of course."

"Yes, we are in love. Why? Do you have some sort of problem with that?"

Rebecca was staring off into space, completely oblivious of the confrontation that was happening.

"Well, you see. Yes. Well, no. Well I have a problem understanding."

"Understanding what?"

"You two being in love."

Everyone on the train, but Rebecca, was now watching these two trains on their path to a head on collision.

"What's wrong with us being in love?"

"Well, it kind of makes no sense. Are you seriously happy with this woman?" Brian asked, completely unaware of how offensive the question was.

"Why the fuck wouldn't I be happy with her? You little punk."

Brian was caught up in the moment. He hoped that this would result in a more in- depth understanding of human attraction.

"I'm not a little punk. I just don't get how two unattractive individuals such as yourselves can partake in the act of sexual intercourse without cringing," Brian said in the most casual of manners.

"What!" The man stood up, ready for a fight.

"Now approaching J .F .K . /U. Mass," said the train. This brought Rebecca out of her trance, and Brian out of danger.

Seeing that Brian was about to be murdered, Rebecca pulled him by the arm onto the train platform. The doors shut and the train, angry man and all, began to move.

"What was that all about?" Rebecca asked stupidly.

"Just a small tiff. Nothing to worry over."

"Alright."

They walked to Rebecca's house hand in hand(Brian saw the great joy it brought Rebecca and decided not to crush it). After walking and partaking in conversation that was far too low for Brian's brain level, they came to Rebecca's house.

"Well here we are," Brian said.

"Yes, here we are."

"Yea."

"Want to come in?"

"No."

"Are you sure?"

Brian was sure.

"Well, say if I were to come in. What would we do?"

"Uh, you see, we can do anything you want. I could blow you. You could finger me. Anything Brian. We could fuck. I've been saving myself for you. So many guys have wanted to fuck me but now you're here and we can fuck. I'd give anything to get fucked by you. Please, let's fuck."

Brian didn't reply. He turned around immediately, and ran home like a frightened child who had just been offered a ride home by a strange man with a large beard.

CHAPTER 5

Brian refused to discuss the date with anyone other than Melvin. His appointment with Hubbard was in a few hours and he was dreading telling her what had happened.

Melvin was very disappointed in Brian. Before, he just thought Brian was odd. Now, however, Melvin looked down on him. If Melvin were in Brian's position the night before this day, he would've acted completely opposite to the way Brian did. He was convinced, as he had been for some time, that Brian was taking his whole life for granted. Melvin was in the real position to be complaining, he knew. Brian was simply overly picky. He wanted nothing but perfection. Melvin, sure that perfection is non existent, was growing more and more tired of this as the time went by. He was not sure he could watch Brian turn one more acceptable girl down.

It was one o' clock on this lovely Saturday afternoon. Brian's appointment with Hubbard was at five. Brian and Melvin were sitting in Melvin's room, doing nothing in particular.

"So, you could've fucked her?" Melvin asked.

"Well, she asked me if I wanted to come in her house. When I asked her what we would do, she started saying a lot of things, things I didn't expect her to say. She told me we could do whatever I wanted. Then, she started going on about sex and how she had saved herself for me and how she didn't want to lose her virginity to anyone else."

"And you turned her down?"

"Yea," Brian said, confused.

"You, you, I hate you. How could you do that?"

"You knew I didn't like her from the beginning. The only reason I agreed to go out with her is because I had no choice."

"Still. Do you have any clue how many guys at school would kill and be killed to get with her?"

"She lacks depth, and plenty of other things too."

"Since when is depth important?"

"I am deep person. How the hell do you expect me to be happy with someone who isn't deep?"

"We're seventeen. The happiness you receive from girls at this time in our life isn't supposed to be a result of intelligent conversation! It's supposed to be from fucking busting on her face while she blows you!"

Brian put his head in his hands for a moment. After the moment had ended, he raised his head and stood up.

"You fucking ignorant, shallow piece of shit! How do you expect that point of view to get you anywhere in life?"

"It works for everyone else," Melvin said. "Now, Brian, if you're looking for depth, why don't you just talk to all the girls who are in the animal lovers' association at school?"

"They're all very ugly."

Melvin was confused.

"I thought you wanted depth."

"Depth isn't everything."

"You just said it was!"

"I said it was important. Just because it's important doesn't mean it's everything!"

The reality of it all was this, Brian was confused with everything, himself above all. What he said meant nothing to him because it didn't make sense to him. He wasn't sure what he wanted, not sure at all. He had a gut feeling that when he came across what he was looking for, he'd know immediately.

"So you want a very good looking, deep girl?" Melvin asked, holding back laughter.

"I guess."

Melvin no longer held back his laughter.

"They don't exist!" Melvin said. His statement was accompanied by hysterical roars.

"Well, I don't know. It seems unlikely that whatever I'm looking for doesn't exist. Why would God put me through that?"

Melvin didn't answer Brian's question. Brian didn't ask why. Nothing occurred but silence, beautiful, productive silence.

"Brian's special. I just realized this now. Maybe he has a better head on his shoulders than the rest of us. He's so reluctant to dive in to anything because he doesn't want to be unhappy in the end. Maybe being unhappy in the beginning is worth being happy in the end. Yes, Brian must be working towards happiness, true happiness. I guess it's a good thing to work towards. Or maybe I'm wrong. He very well just could be a sick, sick asshole with no grip on reality," Melvin said to himself in his head.

I'm a sick, sick asshole with no grip on reality. Brian thought, silently.

"Well, I have that appointment soon. And I want to go home anyways. No offence, but I want to be by myself. I need some thinking time."

"I understand completely. But may I make one small suggestion. I'm sure it'll raise your spirits a little, because it certainly raises mine."

"What?"

"You should really jack off more often."

Brian looked at him, completely confused. He had no clue what to say in response, so he just responded before finding the clue he lacked.

"You jack off?"

"You don't!?"

"Bye."

Brian walked home slowly, sniffing the April air as he did so. It was a nice day. It had been a week of nice days. Brian enjoyed nice weather more than most things.Brian walked through the front door of his house. Edna was in the living room, gleefully dusting the coffee table."Brian, sweetie, hi!"

"Hi, Edna," Brian said, walking toward his room.

"How was your day?"

Brian's bedroom door slammed shut. Edna blew it off and continued dusting.

Brian sat on the edge of his bed, wondering what he would do until his appointment with Hubbard. Without anything to provoke it, his train of thought suddenly took a turn. He began to think about the conversation he and Melvin had just a few minutes ago. Overall it was a pretty common Brian and Melvin conversation. Melvin would yell at Brian, Brian would yell back, and they would both come up with brand new, life altering ideas. These "life altering ideas" no longer altered Brian's life. When you've had so many "life altering ideas" the thrill begins to disappear. It had disappeared for Brian and he still sat on his bed, un- altered life and all.

He was still thinking about his conversation with Melvin. As was just stated, it was a pretty normal conversation for the two of them. The closing statements, however, managed to dig their way deep into Brian's skin. The fact that he was a very abnormal person became very clear to him.

Brian, still seated on the edge of his bed, unzipped his pant and pulled them, and his boxers down to his ankles. He wrapped his hand around his penis and smiled. Just touching it felt good, for he had never touched it with these intentions before.

"What the fuck am I doing?" Brian asked himself out loud. The thought of masturbating hadn't entered his mind until then. He took his hand off of his now erected penis and pulled his boxers and pants up. He tried to get his mind off of the thought he had just had, so he turned his television on and began to watch.

***

Brian sat in the back seat of the car, instead of in front with Edna. He felt dirty. Not dirty in the sense of physical cleanliness, but dirty as in sexually. He was ashamed of what he had thought and contact with Edna would make him feel awkward.

The fact that Brian was very inexperienced in many different aspects of life was becoming very clear to him. Completely oblivious to the fact that just about every male does it, Brian was sure that masturbation was completely immoral. Now that Brian knew that more than a few sinners partake in this activity, he couldn't help but be curious. Curiosity scared him to death. He didn't want to be curious. He was saving himself for someone he loved. Right now, the last person Brian wanted to have his first sexual experience with was himself.

Brian was in a state of deep thought.

"Brian! Brian, we're here," said Edna loudly.

"Where?"

"At Dr. Hubbard's office, silly."

"Is this really necessary?"

"Brian, don't do this now. She is a professional. If she thinks that you need a follow up appointment, I'm sure you need one. Besides, I think it's important she hears about how your recent social status with the females is going."

"I'm sure it is, but I don't want her to know," mumbled Brian.

"She's the reason you went out with that girl in the first place. I know how you are. You wouldn't want to waste your time doing something for no reason, would you?"

"How do you know I didn't do that for myself?"

"I just know. Now let's go."

Brian shook as he walked on the sidewalk. He hated Hubbard. Everything about her made him sick to his stomach. In fact, Hubbard was the kind of person Brian dreaded. She was extremely fat and extremely ugly. She was pushy. Though some points she made may have been good points, the fact that such a woman could come up with good points bothered Brian. Taking orders from Hubbard bothered Brian. Being in Hubbard's presence or even talking about her bothered Brian. Now he had to tell her all about what happened on his date. This was unacceptable.

"The doctor will see you now," said a middle aged woman behind the desk of the waiting room.

Brian passed the front desk and toward the door. He was still shaking. The shakes he had were not shakes of fear, but shakes of disgust. A very fat woman was behind that door, and she had Brian's life in the palms of her plump hands.

Brian opened the door and there she sat. He knew she would be sitting, because he couldn't even picture her standing up without some sort of iron support beam. Her stomach was an avalanche, covering her mountain thighs. Plump was an understatement for the condition her face was in. It was a very fat and very red face. Brian felt a small urge to poke it with a needle to see if it would pop. He decided it was a bad idea, though, because by doing so, he thought, he may get the sweat of her fat body on him.

"Brian., so nice to see you," Hubbard said, rubbing her larger than life stomach.

"Doctor, hi," said Brian.

"How have you been since our last visit?"

"I've been alright, I guess."

"You guess? Guessing isn't a good thing Brian. You can't be all that good if you aren't positive about it."

How dare this mess lecture me? Brian asked himself silently.

"Well maybe I'm not that good."

"Did something happen?"

"No."

"So the date went well?"

"No."

"Did you go on a date like we discussed?"

"Yes."

"So, if you went on a date and it didn't go good, that must mean something happened,"said Hubbard, stroking her double chin.

Brian hated the way Hubbard could get things out of him.

"Okay fine, something did happen," said Brian in a quiet, monotone voice.

"And what was that something?"

"It just didn't go well."

"How didn't it go well?"

"Bad things kept happening."

"You're not getting this, Brian. Right now I would like

you to tell me, in as much detail as possible, what happened on your date."

This was awful and embarrassing. Brian was very reluctant to tell Hubbard what had happened before. But now that he was in her office, sitting in front of her massive body, the amount of his reluctance was multiplied by at least seven. He was nearly positive that there was no way out of this. Trying to find a way out of something that he couldn't find his way out of would only waste time. He wanted Hubbard out of his sight as soon as possible, so he decided to spill his guts.

"Okay, fine. I'll tell you," started Brian. "This is what happened. Well, you see, I tried to do what you told me by saying yes to the first girl who asked me out. The problem with that was that the first girl who asked me out was named Edna. Now as you probably know, Edna is the first name of my mother. Between You and I, I don't like Edna very much. Now when I say I don't like Edna very much I mean my mother, not the Edna who asked me out. Thinking of it though, I don't really like her either. Anyways, I said no to Edna. I could never bear to be in a relationship with someone who had the same first name as my mother. So I said yes to the second girl who asked me out that day. This girl's name was Rebecca. All the guys at my school love her. I, however, haven't the slightest idea why. Well I went to the movies with her. I payed for her ticket, which I knew was the proper thing to do."

"Well that's good, you paying for her ticket I mean," Hubbard said, interrupting.

Brian gave her a dirty look.

"Yea, anyways. It killed me to buy her ticket. You see, I don't like her. That's besides the point though. So we went into the theater to watch the movie. This is where all the serious trouble began. She kept trying to kiss me and other things that

I'd prefer not to tell you. I told her that I wanted her to back off, but she wouldn't listen. This continued throughout the entire movie. Finally, after what seemed like an eternity, the movie ended. I took the train with her. I nearly got killed by a man on the train after only exchanging a few simple words with him. I can hardly believe how sensitive people are these days. Anyways, I walked her to her house. When we got there, she begged me to come in and have sex with her. I didn't reply to her. I just ran away. I was very scared, you see, and didn't know what to do. I don't know if what I did was right and to be completely honest with you, it's been bothering me a lot."

Brian let out a loud and long sigh when he finished speaking. Getting all of that off his chest, to someone other than Melvin, felt surprisingly good to Brian, even if the person he was telling it to was Hubbard.

"Wow. That's quite the story," said Hubbard."

"Yea."

"Hm. If it had been another girl who asked you to come in her house, would you have done it?"

"I can't tell. I don't know any girls who I would want to do anything like that with."

"I see. Well pretend you did know a girl you might want to..."

"I said I don't know any girls like that. I can't pretend! Hubbard, God damn it, why do you have to ask me these stupid fucking questions? Everyone bothers me. I rarely find females attractive. And when I do find them attractive, it all comes to an end once I speak to them. Nothing about anyone is right for me. I'm going nuts and you're certainly not fucking helping me!"

Until this moment, Hubbard thought with all her heart that Brian had a great deal of hope. She thought they he may have a problem that could be easily solved . Now however, she just though he was a horrible human being with no hope of ever recovering from the wretchedness which God had injected him with at birth.

"Well, Brian, I'm sorry you feel that way. That's enough for today. But tell your mother I'd like to speak with her for a few moments when you go out in the waiting room."

Brian left the office and told his mother that Hubbard wanted her.

CHAPTER 6

Brian hated many things, some more than others. High on the list of things he hated was being put in a bad position where he had no say at all. He hated being forced into things he couldn't control. Something had happened, and he hated it with all his being.

A few days after the second appointment with Hubbard, Edna revealed what was discussed between her and Hubbard to Brian. Hubbard explained to Edna that after she and Brian had partook in a deep conversation, she concluded that Brian did, in fact, have a serious problem. Hubbard made it clear to Edna that Brian needed a change in his life. Whatever Brian was looking for did not exist in his life at this moment. Hubbard thought that the best thing to do for Brian was to put him in a new surrounding, giving him the opportunity to meet new people and possibly find what he was lacking in his life.

Edna took Hubbard's advice and turned it into a goal. When Edna McMahon had a goal, every ounce of effort in the woman's body was put into achieving it.

"Brian, Brian, could you come in here for a second. Your father and I would like to speak to you," said Edna. She was seated on the couch of their living room, next to her husband.

Brian's door flew open, hitting the wall. He slowly stepped out of his bedroom. The look on his face was a look of many different feelings. The shape of his lips indicated anger, yet he had very dark bags under his eyes, making him look tired and withdrawn.

"I had a long, hard day at school. I was trying to take a nap," Brian snapped.

"Just sit down, sport. It won't take too long. Plus, it's kind of important," said Harry with his usual light tone.

Brian listened to his father. He walked over to a large and comfortable chair that faced the couch. He sat in the chair and reached his right hand over the side of it. He pulled a lever and his feet flew up. Brian was now reclined, and as ready as he could be to listen to what his parents had to say.

"Yes?"

"Well, your father and I have very good news."

"You do? What is it?"

"Your spring break from school is coming up in what, two weeks?"

"Yea."

"What would you think about taking a cruise to Mexico?"

"I wouldn't think about it. I just wouldn't want to. No thought required," said Brian with his hands folded on his lap.

"But honey, your father and I spent all day yesterday calling travel agencies trying to get a good deal on cruise tickets. After spending hours on the phone, your father found a great deal. We got four tickets."

"Four?"

"Melvin. I know you wouldn't have any fun by yourself. I mean I would like you to talk to the kids on the boat, but I thought it would be nice for Melvin to come along, just in case."

Brian thought to himself as he sat before his parents. He put his parents great care for him into consideration. He thought hard about the fact that they had the best of intentions in doing what they were doing. Even in doing so, Brian still didn't want anything to do with a cruise to Mexico. He wanted to feel bad for his parents, but he just couldn't pull it off.

"I don't want to go. The people around here get under my skin enough. Imagine me with a bunch of Mexicans, who can't speak a word of English, running around me."

Edna and Harry looked at each other. They both nodded their heads simultaneously, then turned back to Brian.

"I don't mean to be pushy," said Harry. "But you're going whether you like it or not. We've already called Melvin about it. He's already all excited."

"Jesus Christ. I hate you two sometimes."

"You really know how to hurt our feelings sometimes, Brian. You can be so unappreciative of the things we do for you. Besides, your doctor said..."

"Hubbard!" Brian interrupted his mother. "What in Jesus Christ's name does that fat mess have to do with this?"

"She suggested to me that you be put in some different surroundings for a while. She thinks you might be happier around people you don't know, as opposed to all the people you already know, and hate."

"My God. I can't believe you let that woman, no, that thing tell you what to do."

Brian dreaded every appointment with Hubbard. He couldn't bare the sight of her. The one hour he had to spend with her each week ruined the entire rest of his week without any problem at all. Now, she had completely manipulated his personal life. He felt violated. He hated feeling violated, as any normal, or even abnormal, person would. Normal violation didn't compare to violation from the likes of Hubbard. It was unbearable.

***

The sun was setting. Brian and Melvin sat on Brian's back porch, just talking. Brian was complaining to Melvin about how he didn't want to go on the cruise. Melvin was trying to explain to Brian that going on the cruise would be good. He wasn't doing a good job of convincing.

"You don't understand, Melvin. I don't want to go. It's such an awful inconvenience. I don't want to leave the country. I'm not the kind of person that leaves the country."

"Brian, come on. Don't you think it would be nice to get away for a while. It's not like you really like anything here."

"So what! I can't believe they actually think that this will help me. It's not like I'm going to see anyone I talk to on the boat ever again."

"I'm sure there will be a lot of hot girls in bathing suits running around," Melvin said with a very toothy smile.

"By now I'd think you'd know I don't care about that. I'm looking for one person. It's not like I have a lot of options. No matter how good looking a girl is, it doesn't matter. I've explained it to you hundreds of times, Melvin. She has to have a combination of everything. She has to be completely compatible with me. Good looks do not equal compatibility."

"They equal a hard erection! As far as I'm concerned, that's just as good. I still think you're nuts though. You have to feel things out. You're never going to find what you're looking for if you don't give things a try first."

Brian had grown sick of saying the same thing over and over again. He was sure that she existed. He knew a moment would come in his life when sparks would fly, when he would say , "this is it, this is the one". He wouldn't need to do any feeling around for that to happen. He was willing to wait, as unfavorable as it was. Brian refused to settle for anything less than flying sparks. He would give no exceptions.

"I just don't want to go. I know I'll have a bad time," said Brian.

"Even if you have nothing to do with any of the girls there, I'm sure you'll have a halfway decent time. We're going to be on a cruise where the sun will always be shining, most likely. I've seen you. You're always smiley when the sun is shining. You're a fool. Overall, Brian, you're a pretty nasty person. But when you're walking down the street with the smell of nature in the air and the sun shining on your head, you seem almost perky."

"You piece of shit. Anything but perky, please. I don't want to be perky."

"Fine. You seem happy anyways. So, if worst comes to worst, you can always prance around the boat and bask in the sun."

Brian wouldn't admit it, but the point Melvin was making excited Brian. For it was true, nice weather was one of the few things Brian honestly enjoyed. When the sun was out and the sky was cloudless, Brian enjoyed walking to the park. On nice days, he would sit there by himself, letting the rays of the golden sun beat down on his head, giving color to his already vibrant head of hair. This was the only thing in the world Brian could think of that could temporarily stop everything. All the burdens and pains that come with living were lifted from Brian, if only for a short period of time. This feeling, and the nature that provoked it, were the only things in the world that Brian had ever considered beautiful.

"Why the hell do you have that big smile on your face?" asked Melvin.

Brian quickly whipped up a frown.

"What in God's name are you talking about?"

"Never mind."

"Fine."

"So, Brian," Melvin said, getting ready to change the subject of their conversation. "Have you taken my advice?"

"What advice are you talking about?"

"You know, the self help thing."

Brian grew awkward.

"Of course not, you sick fuck."

"I am not a sick fuck. I am a normal human being with normal human needs."

"You're a pervert."

"Everyone does it! It relieves frustrations."

"If I wanted to relieve frustrations I'd go to the park and buy some weed."

"It feels good too."

"Leave me alone you fucking asshole! I don't want to. Anyone who has to lose their virginity to their own hand is a pathetic piece of shit."

"We're all pathetic pieces of shit then."

"I'm not."

***

It was a Friday, the last day of school before Spring break began. Brian silently walked down the halls during seventh period. He had asked to go to the bathroom, knowing he could freely walk around. The seventh period class prevented girls from mobbing him. As he walked, he thought. These halls meant nothing to him. The people here meant nothing. Whatever he wanted wasn't here. He began to second guess himself.

He thought this: I'm leaving tomorrow for Mexico, something I've been dreading since I found out about it. Thinking about it now, I'm not so sure why I ever dreaded it in the first place. Nothing here makes me happy. Just because I can't find anything good here, who's to say I can't anywhere else? God wouldn't just whip me on the earth without planning some sort of destiny for me, unless, of course, I'm destined to live a life of complete misery. No! I can't think that way. I'm going to leave this place tomorrow with a smile on my face. Positive thoughts only.

***

Brian arrived at home at approximately three o' clock. He had a smile on his face, the same smile that appeared during the thought session he took in the middle of his school hallway. Once this smile appeared, it didn't go away.

Brian walked into the kitchen where he found Edna. She was pleasantly dancing to the radio and dusting the stove top.

"Good afternoon Edna," said Brian, with an abnormal gleefulness.

"Hello, sweetie. How was school today?"

"Not bad."

"Not bad? Wow. Anyways, are you all ready for the big day tomorrow?"

"Actually, yes. I'm quite excited."

"Excited? That's great! Really, it is. When you tell me that you're excited over something I planned, I really feel like I've accomplished something."

"Good, I'm glad you feel that way, I guess," Brian said, still smiling.

"I'm glad you're glad. Why don't you go pack, sweetie. It's been put off long enough."

"Yea."

The cruise ship to Mexico was not leaving directly from Boston. The McMahon family had to be at Logan Airport by quarter past six A. M. to make the seven o' clock flight to Chicago. From Chicago, they were to take another plane to New Orleans, where they would board the ship. Edna had planned everything down to the last and smallest detail. She wanted the family to be up and ready with time to spare. This was a big event for her and the family and any inconveniences were not acceptable to her.

After Brian had finished packing, he called Melvin to tell him he could come now. Though Melvin lived only a few doors down, Edna thought it would be best if he were to spend the night. That way, he would wake up and get ready with the rest of the family, decreasing the chance of problems.

***

"I can't wait for tomorrow. It's going to be great I tell you, great," said Melvin to Brian. The both of them were sitting in the living room of Brian's house.

"I'm actually pretty excited myself."

"Really? Wow."

"That's what Edna said."

"Well, It makes sense for her to be surprised. But still, even you should be excited. We're leaving our lives for a week. We're going to a place where the weather is nice all the time. I'm sure the food will be good. There'll be entertainment everywhere we go. There'll be people to socialize with. On top of all else, there will be girls."

"Hopefully not as awful as the ones here. I'm really anticipating this cruise. If I come back having gained nothing, I don't know what I'll do. This is my last hope. I was looking forward to getting to live a little."

"That sounds great, getting to live a little. You're so right. We haven't lived. I mean yea, we take up space. We eat, we shit, we piss. Scientifically, yea, we've lived. But have we really lived? I don't really think so. Everything seems so boring. Nothing happens. I want some action, action in more ways than one."

"You're right. Life's been bland. Living a bland life is one thing, but living an unhappy, bland life is another. We deserve more. We'll get more. It won't be fair if we don't."

Brian and Melvin both had very different ideas of what truly living was. Despite this fact, both of their longing desires to live were quite equal. Just the thought of life where happiness was not a stranger gave Brian and Melvin a feeling that any normal human being couldn't put into words. Brian and Melvin knew that they lived to experience happiness. They intended to take this incomprehensible feeling that they got when thinking about their state of happiness and multiply it by a large number. All they had to do was be happy instead of thinking about being happy.

***

Brian lied in his bed. Melvin was on the floor. Edna sent them into the bedroom at ten. They were still wide awake, however. They were having a dry conversation which lacked a real topic.

"Oh yea, Brian. I almost forgot. I brought something I wanted to show you," said Melvin, out of no where.

"Yea. What is it?"

Melvin reached into a duffle bag which lay next to him on the floor. He pulled out a video tape.

"This stuff is really hard to get on D. V. D. when you aren't eighteen yet. I had to settle for a crappy video copy that I bought in the boys' room."

"What is it?"

"You'll see."

Melvin stood up and walked to the T. V. He pushed the video into the V. C. R. that was connected to the T. V. After doing so, he pushed play.

Slow music came from the television speakers. The title, "The Erotic Fudge Shop," appeared on the screen.

"What the fuck is this?" Brian yelled.

"Just sit back and enjoy."

Brian said nothing.

A man and a woman appeared on screen. They began to talk. The conversation didn't last more than a few minutes. Before Brian could realize what was going on, both the man's and the woman's clothing was on the floor of the fudge shop. They were rolling around in the fudge. Looking at the exposed body parts of the woman, Brian's penis grew erect, and his face turned red.

"Melvin, you fucking asshole."

"Come on, be a man."

"Is this some sort of sick plan to make me resort to self help?"

"No."

"Well good. I'm shutting this shit off."

"No!"

Brian got angry. His erection had yet to go down.

"Fine, asshole. I'll leave you alone. Don't you dare make a mess!"

Brian stormed out of his room and ran into the bathroom. He locked the door behind him. He only planned on staying in there for a little while but, being tired, he fell asleep on the bathroom floor.

***

Brian sprung up, hitting his head off of the toilet which he had rolled under in his sleep. Due to the loud knocks, the bathroom door was shaking.

"Who is it?"

"Brian, what in God's name are you doing in there?" asked Edna, with an abnormal sternness.

"I don't know. I came in here last night and I guess I fell asleep."

"Well it's five o' clock in the morning. Everyone else in the house is up. You'd better get up too. We have to be on time!"

Brian stood up from the floor and turned on the shower. He undressed and stepped in. He tried to make it brief, washing only the spots on his body that tended to smell when neglected.

Seeing that Brian didn't leave the bathroom since he had woken up, he had no clothing to put on. He never liked to risk his family seeing him undressed when he went from the bathroom to his bedroom after his shower. He always brought his clothing into the bathroom before getting into the shower.

Brian wrapped a towel around his lower half. He opened the bathroom door just enough to stick his head out. The coast seemed clear. He walked out of the bathroom and into his bedroom without being seen. Melvin was sitting on Brian's bed. He turned to Brian and smiled.

"Get out. I want to change."

"I won't look."

"I spent my whole fucking night sleeping on tiles. It's your fault. I don't feel like looking at you all that much. Get the hell out of my room."

"Fine."

Brian quickly deodorized and put on clothes. He stepped out of his room to be greeted by Harry.

"Good morning, son. You all ready to go?"

"Yes, I am."

Harry smiled.

"Great. We'll be leaving in a few minutes. Why don't you park your pooper on the couch with Melvin. I'm going to be giving your uncle a call in a sec so he can drive us to the airport."

"Okay."

Brian stayed silent throughout the car ride to the airport. Harry and Edna checked the bags in immediately after arriving. Brian and Melvin sat while this was being done.

"Brian?"

"Melvin..."

"Are you pissed at me?"

"You're a pain in the ass. You are, unfortunately, my only form of sanity. I'm not pissed at you."

***

Brian sat by the window and Melvin sat in the middle. A slightly over weight, young, red haired man sat on the out side of the row. Neither Brian nor Melvin had ever flown before. They both had no fear of flying. Why fear something that thousands of people do every day?

Brian remained relaxed throughout the takeoff. He was slightly disappointed. He had assumed all of his life that the take off would be far worse than it actually was.

"Wow, smooth," Brian said to Melvin.

"Yea," interrupted the over weight, red haired man. "I've been flying since I was a kid. It's no big deal at all."

"Yea, thank you," Brian replied in an intentionally mean tone of voice.

About five minutes after the take off, a slight discomfort

came into being in both of Brian's ears. Ten minutes after the take off, the slight discomfort had turned into a sharp pain.

"Melvin," Brian said, holding both of his ears.

"Yea?"

"Are you getting this weird feeling in your ears?"

"Yea. Kind of."

"Just kind of? Both of my ears are killing me."

The red haired man turned to Brian.

"Your ears are popping. That's what happens when you fly in a plane. It's the air pressure," said the red haired man.

"How do I make it go away?"

"I have some Tylenol."

The fat man reached into his pocket and pulled out a small bottle of Tylenol. He opened the bottle and shook two pills into the palm of his hand. He offered them to Brian. Brian looked at the pills. They were moist with the sweat of the man's palm.

"I think I'll survive," said Brian, rolling his eyes.

Sleeping must be better than being awake and in pain. Brian closed his eyes and pushed his chair back. With the exception of his ear pain, he was comfortable. Suddenly his chair was pushed back into its original position. Brian thought that maybe there was just something wrong with the chair. He pushed it back again and, again, it was moved forward by some unknown force. Brian turned around. The unknown force was a small, blonde boy, who was no older than five years of age.

"I'm trying to sleep you little prick!"

A very muscular man who was sitting next to the boy gave Brian a nasty look.

"Yell at my son again and I'll punch you so hard that your eyeballs will come out your ass crack, you little prick."

Brian said nothing. He turned around, not daring to push his chair back again.

***

Brian sat in his chair, wide awake and in agony. Both Melvin and the red haired man had dozed off. The red haired man had begun to snore very loudly quite some time ago. Brian was on his wit's end until he noticed a couple seated in the row across from his. An immediate feeling of disgust came over him. The woman was wearing a sleeveless shit. He upper arms were very flabby. The flab jiggled every time she moved her arm. She had short hair that was a very bland shade of brown. The man had very short hair. Having such a badly textured head of hair, he wouldn't have been able to manage the hair if it was anything but short. The grossness of the man's hair, however, was nothing compared to his arms, which weren't visible due to the large masses of bushy, fur- like hair on them. To top all flaws off, on the lap of the woman was an infant.

"My God," said Brian.

The fact that these two people had to have sex to produce this child was too much. Brian grew scared. Brian had to find "her". If he didn't, he was scared that he would stoop to the level of resorting to someone he didn't care for.

CHAPTER 7

After waiting in line for nearly an hour with their future, temporary neighbors, the McMahon family boarded the boat. After being given their key-cards, they were directed to their rooms.

Brian and Melvin shared a room right next to Edna and Harry's room. Melvin sat on his bed and watched the television with the volume down low. Brian tried to sleep, which was the only thing he wanted to do after the plane ride, but couldn't on account of the fact that his parents were ranting and raving, very loudly, about how great the boat was. Through the wall, he could hear them as clearly as if they were standing over him.

Brian, still lying in his bed, heard a door slam shut. He looked up and saw that Melvin was still pleasantly sitting on his bed. With the slamming of the door also came the silence of Edna and Harry. Brian assumed they went to explore the boat and thought no more of it after that.

Not five minutes into the slumber, which Brian had achieved, there was a knock at the door.

"What the fuck," Brian mumbled, still half asleep.

Melvin got up from his bed and opened the door. It was a tall, voluptuous, blonde woman. She was wearing a name tag that said "Gerta".

"Hi?" said Melvin.

"Hello my dear, My name is Gerta. I'm going to be your cleaning lady throughout your stay here."

"Hey Brian! Come here and meet Gerta!"

"Wait," Brian mumbled.

Brian rolled out of his bed and walked to Melvin and Gerta.

"Hi Gerta, where are you from?"

She gave him an odd look, then smiled.

"I'm from Albania."

"I hear Albanians really know how to keep a clean place," Brian said, and threw himself back into the bed.

"Well, I don't know about all of them, but I'm certainly good at it. I will come by twice a day to clean the room for you two. If you don't want me to clean at a certain time, just put that little "do not disturb" card by the doorknob in the key slot. When I see this, I will know to come back later."

"Well this is good," said Melvin, extending his hand for a shake. "It's been a pleasure meeting you, Gerta."

"Yes, yes, a great pleasure. You two are seated a table 18 at the second dinner, which is at eight o' clock. If you don't feel like going to that, there is also a buffet every night. Yes, well goodbye. And don't hesitate to make a mess. I am a professional."

With that, Gerta left.

***

Brian and Melvin spent the next few hours in their cabin. During this period of time, Edna and Harry returned from their ship exploration. They knocked at the cabin door, waking Brian up. They rambled on about how beautiful the boat was. "You guys should really leave your room soon," claimed Edna. It sounded so very tempting. But Brian was completely drained, and Melvin wasn't about to wander the boat aimlessly by himself.

After Edna and Harry's drop- in, Brian dozed off again. An hour into this doze, he was woken up by a voice that came from the speaker of their cabin television.

"Good evening everybody. This is your captain speaking. I hope you've all made yourselves comfortable. Well, we've been moving about a half hour now. In approximately fifteen minutes, all passengers must report to deck five for a routine safety demonstration. Thank you for your time and enjoy your stay on , "The Prancer of the Seas"."

Brian rolled out of his bed and hit the floor. He grabbed on to the night stand that was in between his and Melvin's bed and pulled himself up into a standing position.

"Jesus Christ," Brian said, shaking his head in an attempt to wake himself up. "Melvin, I don't know what the hell's come over me. I'm so friggen tired."

"Hm, well, I don't know. I'm sure you'll be fine once you're up and walking around. I say right after the demonstration we take a nice walk around the ship. Maybe we can meet some people," said Melvin.

"Sounds like a plan. Melvin, please, don't allow me to be too shallow. Force me to talk to people. I want to have fun. I don't know how to go about it. Force me into it. If I show signs of holding back, kick me in the crotch with all your might."

"I'll make sure tears flow from your eyes."

"You're a pal," Brian said.

***

Brian and Melvin didn't speak through the demonstration. The simply followed what was being demonstrated. They anticipated the demonstration's end with an abnormal excitement. When it was over, they quickly ran off.

They immediately went to the top pool deck, seeing as

that's where they thought all the people worth socializing with would be. Brian, now awake, walked with Melvin. He made Melvin stop, because he wanted to look over the rail. The sun was setting. Brian looked out. There was no land visible. He simply saw the navy blue sky meet the aqua green water, with half of a pinkish- orange sun in between. He breathed in, appreciating the fresh, clean air; not like he was used to breathing while in the city. All this, on top of the perfect temperature, made Brian smile. The smile was so wide that it made him feel dumb and vulnerable.

"Wow, it's really nice up here, isn't it?" Brian asked Melvin.

"Yea," Melvin said, not seeming to appreciate what Brian had just been admiring.

Brian ran his fingers through his hair.

"Brian, over there. There's a big group of kid's. Let's go over there."

"No."

"Son of a bitch, I'll kick you so hard you won't be able to get it up for the rest of your life!" Melvin yelled, not very seriously.

"Fine, fine."

Brian and Melvin walked toward the group. The people apparently saw them coming. They began yelling for them to come over. Growing closer, Brian saw that there were eight kids. Two of them were short, fat, twin brothers. There was a tall boy with dark hair and acne. There were two blonde boys, who had no aspects that stood out in particular. There was a short fat girl, a tall blonde girl with breasts that were far too big for the rest of her body, and a red haired girl who was in the middle of tall and short. She wasn't quite skinny, but not chubby either.

"Hi!" Melvin exclaimed to the group.

"Hello," said the tall boy with acne. "What's up?"

"Nothing is up," said Brian. "Not with us anyways, how about you?"

Melvin, happy that Brian decided to speak, smiled.

"Nothing here. We all just met about an hour ago. My name's Mike. The two boys who look the same, they're Anthony and Adam. Those two are Jim and Tom," Mike said, pointing. "And the girls. The red headed one, her name's Dana. The Blonde one is Leah. And the shortest one, she's Susan."

"Well, hi," said Melvin. "I'm Melvin, and this is my cousin Brian."

"Hi Melvin. Hi Brian," said all the boys in the group simultaneously.

"Hi Brian!" said all the girls, with young, naive smiles on their faces.

As much as he wanted to, Brian found none of the girls attractive. But they seemed nice, and at this point, nice was enough to keep him from walking away.

Brian wondered where they were all from. He was reluctant to become too friendly with people who he would never see again. If he knew that any of them were from somewhere distant, he would naturally distance himself from them. The last thing he wanted to do was to distance himself from anyone who might help him be happy.

"We were all just going back to my room. We're going to be spending the next week together. I think some time to get to know each other would be good. Do you guys want to come?" Mike asked Brian and Melvin.

Brian and Melvin exchanged glances.

"I don't see why not," said Melvin.

Brian was one of the first to enter the room, so he got to sit on one of the beds. All the girls in the group crowded around him. They all tried to make conversation with him, giggling as they did so.

All of them, in an attempt to get to know each other, partook in conversation. They covered many topics. They told embarrassing stories about themselves and their friends back home. Brian hoped that when they told stories of home, none of them would actually say where home was. None of them did.

"I snuck some weed on the boat with me," said Mike, an hour into the conversation. "Do you guys want any?"

"Sure," everyone but Brian said.

"Brian?" Melvin said.

"I don't know."

"Come on."

In a week, Brian would be back home, probably hating his life.

"I don't know what I was thinking, sure."

"Good, I have a really nice pipe," Mike said.

The pipe was passed around in circles. After four or five puffs, Brian felt out of it. It was a good kind of out of it. He felt free.

"This is awesome, you guys," Brian said. "Why didn't anyone make me do this sooner?"

"I don't know," said one of the fat twins.

"You could feel better you know. I have a flask on vodka in my bag too. You seem like a nice boy. Are you interested?" Mike asked.

Brian got the feeling that he was being spoken down to. In the frame of mind that he was in, however, he didn't let it bother him.

"Yes, do me a favor. I need a favor. I've been needing favors all my fucking life," Brian said, laughing hard.

Everyone in the room looked at him as if he were insane.

Brian took a few large swigs. He thought it tasted awful. He wanted to feel good, though. Brian and Melvin shared the last few sips.

Brian was standing up now, walking about in the room, speaking nonsense to everyone in the room and cracking up laughing. He was high, drunk, and vulnerable. Every female in the room thought about taking advantage of him.

"I have to piss like a fucking race horse!" yelled Brian. He stumbled and walked through the first door he came across. That door wasn't the bathroom door. It was the room door. Brian was now stumbling about in the hallway. Everyone he was with was too high to care.

***

Brian felt like he had been wandering for hours. He wanted to go back to his room, but didn't know how to get there. He looked straight ahead of him. In the distance he could see a figure coming toward him. He stumbled forward quickly, curious of who the figure was. It was an angel. A blonde angel. She was beautiful. Brian smiled at her.

"There you are!" he yelled.

"Yes, here I am."

"I've been looking for you for the longest time. I want you to do what you want with me."

Brian extended his hand and she took it, then led him away.

CHAPTER 8

It was the next morning. Melvin had just woken up in his bed. At some point the night before, he managed to find his way back to his and Brian's cabin. Melvin stood up, then sat back down. He felt very sick. He looked in the bed next to him. It was empty. The empty bed provoked vague memories of Brian leaving their friend's room the night before, and not coming back. Melvin knew that in the state he was in last night, he could have easily been taken advantage of. He also knew that Brian took in more substances than he did, probably making him even easier to be taken advantage of.

After an hour of lying in his bed, feeling sick, Melvin managed to get up. He left the cabin with the intention of finding Brian.

His first stop was Mike's room. He knocked hard at the door. Mike answered. He looked awful.

"Hey, sorry to wake you. You haven't seen Brian by any chance, have you?" asked Melvin.

"No man. Sorry. Haven't seen him since last night."

"Do you think any of the other guys might know where he is?"

Mike laughed. "No, I don't think so. They're all still in my room, and they're all in a dead sleep."

"Shit. Well, I guess I'll have to go look for him then. Christ only knows where he ended up last night."

"Only Christ. But yea, If a while goes by and you still

haven't found him, just come back. I'm sure in an hour or so most of us will be okay. We'll help you look."

"Yea, thanks," Melvin said nervously.

This was awful. Though Melvin and Brian were both two awkward, inexperienced young men who both longed for thrill in their lives, Melvin had a much better grip on reality. Though Melvin was a stranger to reality and the effects it had on people, he thought about it often and knew a great deal about it also. Brian, on the other hand, only thought about things and how they might appease to him, not how real things might actually affect him in real life. The blueprints of Brian's brain had been written in only black and white ink. Everything was either this way or that way, right or wrong. Melvin's mind was in full color. He knew the ways of the world much better than Brian did. Knowing the ways of the world, he thought Brian could be in a great deal of trouble.

Melvin took the elevator up to the top pool deck. Despite the fact that Brian was missing, he couldn't help but smile when he saw and felt the beautiful sun. He took a moment to appreciate this glowing yellow orb of warmth that heated his shoulders, then regained his seriousness.

Melvin carefully scanned every single spot on the pool deck. With the exception of a few over weight, middle aged men with man- boobs who were sunbathing, there was no one on the pool deck.

Melvin sighed a sigh of despair and got back on the elevator. When the elevator stopped at the fifth floor, a large family got on. Behind them was a young man whose eyes seemed to penetrate all concrete things that existed. This young man was Brian.

"Brian! Where the fuck have you been!?" yelled Melvin.

Each member of the family gave him a dirty look.

Brian stared off, not answering Melvin.

"Brian!"

Melvin shook him hard.

"What, what? Melvin, there you are! Where the fuck have you been?" asked Brian obliviously.

"You're the one who disappeared."

"I'm so confused."

"Let's go back to our room."

Melvin brought Brian back to their room. Melvin sat Brian down on his bed and began questioning him.

"Last night, what happened?"

"Well, I remember going to Mikes room with you. Then I smoked and drank. I tried to go to the bathroom. That's where I draw a blank."

"Uh- huh. How did you end up on the fifth floor?" asked Melvin.

"That's the most confusing thing. I woke up in some cabin I haven't seen before. All my clothes were on the floor. And there was a girl sleeping next to me. Here clothes were on the floor too."

"Oh my God, man. You got some action last night! And you don't even fucking remember it!" Melvin said, in hysterics.

"Shut up you asshole. It's not funny. I didn't come here for a bunch of meaningless love. I'm so scared," Brian said, with his face in the palm of his hand.

"Was she good looking?" asked Melvin, giggling.

"She was an angel. She was gorgeous. I couldn't believe my eyes."

"So why the hell are you complaining?"

"I don't know her!"

"Just go to her room."

"I don't remember the number."

"You're an idiot."

"I'm sorry, Melvin. She was beautiful though. I'm going to find her, and I'm going to know her. Maybe life's finally throwing me some good cards. Maybe life is throwing me life the way it's meant to be experienced. I really want to live, Melvin, now more than ever," said Brian, running his fingers through his, now greasy, locks of hair.

***

Both Brian and Melvin were as clean as can be. They both bathed and got dressed for dinner. The reason for this was that Edna and Harry had made a dinner date. On the flight to New Orleans, while Brian and Melvin were dealing with the large, red- haired man who snored, Edna and Harry were socializing. They acquainted themselves with a family who was also from Boston. This family was the Parker family. According to Edna and Harry, Tom and Jan parker were a very nice, down to earth couple. The reason Brian and Melvin were all spiffed up was not for Tom and Jan, but for their daughter, Ashley.

Brian sat Harry down and asked him about Ashley Parker. Harry told him that she was an extremely attractive young girl, and she seemed nice too. Harry told Brian that he wouldn't understand it if Brian didn't like her. Brian then told Melvin this bit of information. Now, both Brian and Melvin had their hopes up. Brian was hoping for a beautiful, deep young woman who would provide him with a natural high every time he was in her presence. Melvin, on the other hand, was looking for a very easy young lady who was up for anything, and could go for hours at a time.

"I still can't get over last night," said Brian to Melvin. They were sitting in their cabin, a half hour before they were supposed to have dinner with the Parkers.

"I know. We never really got to discuss it. Do you have any clue what happened at all?" asked Melvin.

"I don't even remember meeting her. All I know is that I woke up in the same bed as her, and I wasn't wearing any clothes when I woke up. You don't think I had sex with her, do you?"

"You asked that like it's not possible. I'd hate to break it to you, Brian, but it's pretty safe to assume that you are no longer a virgin."

"Shit, I was thinking that, then I decided it was a bad thing to think."

"Come on. You have to be realistic sometimes. Now is not a time to be unrealistic about things. Maybe you'll find her and she'll be a great girl and you'll live happily ever after. That's the way you want it, isn't it? Well yea any ways, we'll have plenty of time for discussing after dinner. Now let's worry about Ashley Parker. I'm sure you'll find you're blonde angel though."

"But what if..."

"No!" exclaimed Melvin loudly. "No what if's aloud, not on this boat."

***

Such a pretty picture, Edna, Harry, Melvin, and Brian, all walking down the hall together. They were, of course, on their way to meet the Parkers for dinner. Edna and Harry were all excited. They loved having buddies to invite over on Friday nights to play board games with. They hoped that this dinner would result in other dinners, which would result in a long time friendship. Melvin and Brian were trying to envision what Ashley would be like. Melvin had his mind completely focused on Ashley, who he had yet to meet. But Brian's mind seemed to be scattered around in different places. Brian looked for to meeting Ashley Parker with great anticipation. At the same time, however, he kept thinking about the blonde angel. If he met Ashley and they fell head over heels for each other and lived happily ever after for the rest of their lives, that wouldn't be a half bad thing. But if that were to happen, that would destroy any hope of having anything to do with the blonde angel who, Brian was pretty sure, he had lost his virginity to. Brian's virginity was important and he was confused.

For a brief moment Brian became religious. Brian spoke of God often, but never once thought about praying. Now, he began to pray to God. This kind of prayer was not the typical, already written prayer such as the Our Father or the Hail Mary, but more of a one way conversation with God. Brian asked God to make everything work out. Then he thought: Well, If I talk to Ashley Parker, What if God says, "No! Now you can't have anything to do with the blonde angel. Looks like you really screwed things up, Brian." But what if God lets me find the blonde angel, and she's not that great, and then, just because I went and found her, God won't let me have anyone else?

Realizing that he was being ridiculous by overanalyzing all of this, Brian broke out into laughter. Everyone stared at him. He thought this: I'll trust your judgement, God. After all, you are God.

They sat at a table in the open buffet room, which was where they were meeting the Parker family. The McMahons hated eating second dinner in the dining room. They were seated with a family of annoying born- again Christians who they hated.

The Parker family had yet to arrive.

"Wow, honey, this is odd. They didn't strike me as the type of family who would be late for anything," said Edna to Harry.

"Well I'm sure they'll be right along."

Brian and Melvin exchanged looks. They both knew what each other was thinking, because they were both thinking the exact same thing: The family better hurry their asses up so we can see their friggen daughter.

"Oh look, there they are!" yelled Edna excitedly. She stood up and began to wave.

Brian and Melvin both saw Tom and Jan Parker. Between their steps, they saw bits and pieces of a blonde figure walking behind them. After five seconds of walking behind Tom and Jan, the girl pushed through the space in between her parents, and began to walk in front of them.

"Wow, she's really hot," Melvin whispered in Brian's ear.

Brian didn't speak. He was staring at her.

"My God. I don't think you get it. I need a cold shower, right now," whispered Melvin.

Brian still remained silent.

Tom took a seat next to Harry and Jan sat next to Edna. Ashley took the one seat the was left. It was in between Edna and Melvin. Melvin looked at Brian and smiled, turning beet red as he did so. Brian did not notice the smile Melvin gave him. He was still silent and was still staring at Ashley. She noticed him staring at her and she smiled. Behind her luscious, full lips were flawless teeth. They were a shade of white that could only be described as blinding.

"Uh, hey there. How are you doing?" asked Melvin.

"I'm fine. You?" asked Ashley, giggling with femininity.

"I'm good, better now that you're here," Melvin said, grinning and bobbing his head like a complete imbecile. "Brian, are you planning on talking at all?"

Brian stood up abruptly.

"I have to pee!"

Everyone at the table immediately stopped talking. They looked at him and scratched their heads.

"You have to pee, honey?" asked Edna.

"I mean well yea," Brian said, realizing that he was causing a small scene. "Well. I didn't mean to be rude about it. But Melvin, I need your help."

"You need Melvin's help peeing?" asked Harry with an annoying chuckle.

"Listen, all you need to know is that Melvin and I need a moment alone. Come on, Melvin."

Brian got up from his chair and began to walk toward the buffet room door.

"I have no idea what he wants," Melvin said with his eyebrows raised. "Excuse me."

***

"What the fuck are you doing, you fucking idiot? Are you trying to make mother fucking fools out of us!?" Melvin yelled as soon as he saw Brian in the bathroom.

"Melvin, just shut the hell up for a God- damned minute. You're so fucking obnoxious sometimes, Jesus. Just listen. That's her!"

"Who's her?"

"She's her."

"Who's she?"

"Ashley!"

"Ashley's who?"

"The girl I woke up in bed with!"

"You lucky fuck! I hate you."

Brian was ecstatic. He was dancing around the men's room, singing.

"This is it, Melvin. This is it! Look at what's happening.

She just came to me again. And she's from Boston. And look how beautiful she is. This is it, she is her. I'm so happy!"

Brian shed a few tears. Melvin sneered.

"Yea, wow. Isn't this good. Can we go back to the table now? I'm sure your soul mate is getting all antsy for you."

"Yes! Let's go back."

***

Brian and Melvin sat back down at the table. Brian smiled at Ashley. She smiled back.

"I'm sorry about that, everyone. There was something important I forgot to do," Brian said.

"Uh- huh. Important enough to be rude?" Edna asked.

"Important."

The rest of the dinner went smoothly. The conversation between the two married couples was non- stop. During the dinner, they had made plans with each other for each remaining day of the cruise, and were already making plans for after they returned to Boston. Melvin and Brian partook in some small talk with Ashley. Glances and eye- winks were exchanged by Brian and Ashley throughout the dinner. They both knew that this was not their first encounter and they both knew that it would not be their last.

The dinner was over. Edna and Harry were off to visit the casino with Tom and Jan. Brian and Ashley started talking with each other outside of the dinner hall. Melvin stood next to Brian.

"Hey, I'm really glad to see you again," Brian said, putting his arm around Ashley. He smirked at Melvin.

Brian didn't know this girl, but he had never been happier to see someone in his entire life.

"Yea. I'm really glad to see you too. Hey, do you want to come back to my room with me?"

"When?"

"Right now. We can just hang out. I don't have any plans at all, and the other night, I had a blast."

"Yea, sure. Melvin, you don't mind, do you?" Melvin sighed. "Oh come on, go hang out with Mike and them. I'm sure they're doing something constructive that you can join in on," Brian said, then he laughed.

Melvin rolled his eyes.

"Uh- huh," Melvin mumbled.

"Great. Let's go," Brian said happily. He took Ashley by the hand. Holding her hand made him feel warm and mushy. He loved it.

Ashley led the way to her room. Brian smiled a foolish smile, and then he thought this: Wow, ha ha. This is great. She makes me feel so happy. I mean look at her, she's great. She's what I need. I feel so warm. There is a tingle in my chest, a fucking tingle. A God- damned tingle must mean something. But I don't know her. Shit, I'm fucking naive. No, no. She's great. I don't need to know her. I'm having that feeling I've been waiting for. All I need is the feeling, all I need is the tingle in my chest.

Brian sat on the bed in Ashley's cabin. He looked around and thought about the other morning when he woke up in this bed, next to sleeping Ashley, who he didn't know. He remembered how pretty and innocent she looked in her sleep. It made him smile and run his fingers through his hair. He wanted to prance, but didn't want to make a fool of himself.

"So, you're from Boston. I didn't know that."

"Yea. Isn't that good? We can see each other all the time when we go home."

"Yea. And our parents really hit it off. This is really weird, like fate brought us together," Brian said, letting out a happy breath.

"Fate, what are you talking about?" Ashley asked as she pulled her shirt over her head.

It occurred to Brian that maybe she wasn't that deep of a thinker. It was okay. Look at all the signs. Whether Ashley realized it or not, God meant for them to be together. Plus, there was the tingle. Brian put all his faith in the tingle, not God. But whoever was out there, God, or fate, or even Buddha, meant for them to be together.

"Why are you taking your shirt off?"

"Don't you want me to have my shirt off when we do this?"

"Do what?"

"Get down and dirty, you know. You had no problem doing it the other night. What, don't you like my tits?"

"Yes, uh, you have very nice tits, Ashley. But, I don't know you really well. Maybe we should talk for a while, maybe cover the basics."

"We have plenty of times for that. I'm in the mood. Come on," Ashley said, sitting on Brian's lap in straddle position.

She put her tongue in his mouth and began to move it around. At first, he let it happen. Confused, he began to caress her tongue with his. This was the first time he could remember ever kissing a girl.

She slowly moved down to Brian's lower half. She began to pull his pants down, then she began to pull her own down.

"What are we doing?"

"It."

"We're doing it?"

"Yea, like last night."

"Is 'it' all you're about."

"It's all I'm about right now. Don't worry. Just let your animal instincts flow out of you."

Brian stood up and pulled his pants up. Naked Ashley fell over.

"I'm sorry. I forgot something. I have to go. I'll see you later," Brian said, walking quickly to the door.

"What. No Come back!"

"I'm real sorry," Brian said. He opened the door and walked out.

***

Brian stormed into his cabin. Melvin was lying on his bed, sleeping.

"God damn it!" Brian screamed, waking Melvin up.

"What the fuck? What's wrong?"

"I lost my innocence, my fucking innocence to this girl. I lost what I've been preserving forever. All for nothing. Meaningless! Fucking meaningless!"

"She's hot."

"NOOOOOOOOOO!"

Brian punched a mirror that was above his bed. He broke it and his hand began to bleed.

"AHHHHH!" he screamed, and threw himself to the floor, sobbing like a child.

CHAPTER 9

The boat rocked in the night. Brian, having been thrown out of bed in his sleep by the rocking, woke up on the floor. He stood up, but lost his balance and fell to the floor when the boat shook again. He yawned and rubbed his eyes, then he remembered what had happened the night before and how much he hated his life.

"Fuck," he mumbled to himself.

Just then, Brian was nearly killed by a flying Melvin. Melvin had just rolled out of bed due to the rocking. He woke up also.

"What the hell's going on?"

"I don't know. I rolled out of bed and woke up. Everything's rocking. I guess we're on rough waters."

"Uh- huh. How are you?"

Brian laughed. "Awe- struck, Melvin. It was all meaningless. Meaningless!"

"Okay," Melvin said, wishing he had never asked Brian how he was. "Well we're both wide awake. I say we go see what's making all the rocking."

"Fine," Brian said, rubbing his eyes again.

When Brian and Melvin went through one of the doors to the pool deck, they were greeted by a fleet of heavy rain drops. The sky was a dark shade of grey. Wind was blowing at high speeds. Brian and Melvin, both already soaked, began to walk around.

"Another sign from God," Brian said.

"What?"

"Another sign from God. Now he's telling me , 'Ha! I tricked you. This is how your life is really going to be, cold and grey!' It really sucks."

"You suck. You had one bad experience. I'd give my left nut and half my right for a friggen bad experience like yours. Let's go back inside the boat, I'm cold."

They walked through an automatic door and into the elevator hall. A middle aged woman came stumbling by them. She gave both of them a look, as if she had something important to say, then she vomited on the maroon carpet in the hall.

"Oh, uh, Jesus, I'm real sorry. I'm just not used to..." She vomited again. Sweat was running down her forehead. "I'm not used to this sort of rocking. I'm sea sick. I'm sorry you guys had to see that."

"No, don't worry about it," Melvin said.

He looked at Brian. Brian was sweating himself, and his skin had an odd discoloration.

"Are you okay, honey?" asked the vomit woman.

Brian looked at her, then spewed all over her shirt.

"Oh, honey. You're not so well yourself. We should all go back to our cabins..." she puked.

"Are you okay?" asked Melvin, concerned but holding back laughter.

"Yes, just nauseous."

Brian looked like he was about to pass away.

"Come on now, let's get him in bed this instant. He looks worse than I feel," said the vomit woman.

Together, Brian, Melvin, and the vomit woman walked down the halls. All three of them were stumbling and falling all over the place. Brian and the woman took turns vomiting on the carpet as they walked. Melvin tried not to laugh at both of their vomiting spells.

Melvin and the woman got Brian into bed.

"Thank you so much," Brian mumbled. "I don't know you, but you've been really kind."

"Oh, think nothing of it," the woman said, walking out the door of the cabin. She smiled at Brian, then blew chunks.

"Alright," Melvin said, standing up. "I'm going to walk her to her room to make sure she's okay."

"No, I'm fine dear."

"It's the least I can do. Let's go."

Melvin returned about ten minutes later to find Brian still in bed, green skin and all. "Wow, she puked a good three times while we walked to her cabin. I don't know where the hell it all came from."

"I'm sure every bit of puke that came out of her body was filled with nothing but pure love," Brian groaned.

"You're odd."

"Whatever. I don't see how you're fine and I'm practically on my death bed."

"Strong stomach I guess."

The conversation was interrupted by a voice coming out of the television speakers.

"This is your captain speaking. I hope your all enjoying your stay with us thus far. I apologize for the ship's rocking. It seems that we've encountered a little storm. We should be out of it within an hour or so. In the meantime, you should all start getting ready for shopping and attractions. Tomorrow morning we will be docking at our first stop, Cozumel! And don't forget, tomorrow night is formal night on the ship. Get you're suits and dresses ready for portraits taken by our professional photographers! Thank you."

As the captain gave his closing words, the ship tilted to the side, and Brian rolled out of bed, hitting the floor with a loud thud.

"Ehh," he moaned.

***

Brian was lying in his bed, as he had been for the past three hours. He was alone. Melvin had grown sick of listening to Brian's moaning, so he went off to find Mike and the rest of the substance abusers.

The rocking had pretty much died down. Brian felt a little bit better. But because he had absolutely nothing else to do, and because he still felt the slightest bit nauseous, and because he still hated his life, he decided to remain in his bed.

He was looking at the show schedule on the television screen. He saw that a comedian was set to perform later in the night.

"Maybe I'll go to that. It might get my mind off of things," he said to himself.

There was a knock at the door.

"Who is it?" Brian yelled from the bed.

"It's your mother. Let me in!"

"I'm sleeping Edna!"

"If you're sleeping, then how in God's sweet name are you talking to me?"

"You! You pain! Wait a sec," Brian said, grinding his teeth so hard that it hurt.

Brian walked to the door and opened it.

"What!?"

"Honey, hi. How are you feeling?"

"Shitty."

"Don't say shitty, honey. Say poopy. Your father and I are

going out with that nice couple we had dinner with the other night. Would you and Melvin like to come along? There's a magician performing. It might be kind of neat."

"No magicians are neat. It's all fake. Besides, Melvin is off somewhere and I'm sick."

"Sick? Sick how?"

"The boat rocking got me sick. I've been puking all day. And when I haven't been puking, I've been in bed, feeling like I have to puke."

"Oh, sweetie, I'm sorry. You know, it's really a pity, their little daughter is coming along. I guess she was really looking forward to seeing you again. Oh well, I guess she'll have to deal."

"I guess she will," Brian said, running his hand through his sweaty hair.

***

It was now three o' clock in the after noon. It had been about two hours since Edna's visit and magic show invitation. Brian had long since fallen asleep. It was the first time that day that Brian wasn't disturbed by something. It was also the last time that day.

The cabin phone rang, waking Brian up out of his dead sleep. He rolled out of his bed, blanket still on him, and crawled to the corner of the room where the phone was.

He picked it up.

"Hello?"

"Hi sweetie!"

"Who the hell is this?"

"It's your mother, silly. What are you doing?"

"Well I was sleeping, Edna, until you woke me up that is."

"I'm sorry I_"

"What are you calling me for?" Brian snapped viciously.

"I am at in the Parkers' room with your father. We all are coming back to our room. All the good bars are crowded."

"What the hell does this have to do with me?"

"Ashley's coming back with us too. She wants to see you. I told her she could hang out with you while we adults do our own thing. We're right upstairs, so expect a knock at your door any minute," Edna said. Brian knew he couldn't argue.

"Um, alright."

"Bye honey."

"Fuck!" Brian yelled as he hung up the phone.

Brian panicked. He ran around his cabin in small circles, screaming out profane words as he did so. There was no possible way he could see Ashley. Without putting anyone but his own feelings into consideration, he stormed out of the cabin.

He ran down the hall, praying every moment that he wouldn't bump into his parents and the Parkers. He got to the hall where the elevators and main staircase were. He stopped and thought for a moment. He knew Edna well, and she always chose an elevator over a flight of stairs, regardless of how short a distance up or down she was traveling. Edna had a way with her words when it came to convincing others to do something she wanted. He was sure that they would be coming down in the elevator, so he ran for the stairs.

Brian ran up the stairs without stopping, not even to breathe. He did not know why, but his destination was the top floor pool deck. When he came to the seventh floor, he bumped into Melvin, who was wandering about aimlessly.

"Brian, oh wow, you're better!"

"Yea."

"I have to tell you," Melvin said, cracking up laughing. "I

was just in Mike's room. His cleaning lady made a goose out of his towel, a fucking goose!" Melvin laughed even harder. "Let's stay away from our room for a while, maybe Gerta will make us a goose too! Maybe even an elephant!"

"You're high, and I can't talk. I have to go," Brian said, and began running up the stairs again.

Brian could hear Melvin yelling at him to come back. He ignored the yells, for he was in no mood for Melvin, or anyone for that matter.

Brian reached the pool deck. As a result of all the running, he was breathing very heavily. He pushed through a door that led to the outside. It had stopped raining, but the sky was still grey, and the ground still damp. There were few people on the pool deck. For no apparent reason, except for a strange and strong urge, Brian went up the stairs that led to the upper deck over the pool deck.

He reached the upper deck and immediately went to the edge of the deck and looked out into the ocean. It was completely calm now. He looked up at the sky. There was a small opening in the clouds. The sun shined through it brightly, hitting Brian in the face.

"A sign from God. No! No more signs from God. Those are what's getting me into all this shit!" Brian yelled.

Just as he finished making a statement to no one, the boat tilted abruptly, throwing Brian across the deck and over the rail. His body hit a damp chair on the pool deck with a loud smack.

***

Brian came out of the state of unconsciousness that he had fallen into when he hit the deck. He did not open his eyes, but he could smell the sea and hear the air. Brian felt warmth on his body and orange light was penetrating his thin eye lids. He knew that the sun was out.

Brian opened his eyes. A blurry, thin figure with long hair stood over him. Blinding light surrounded the figure on all sides.

"Shit, I'm dead!" he screamed out.

"No, you idiot, you're not dead. You nearly killed me though," said the figure.

"Who the hell are you?"

"Why the hell do you care? Get up."

Brian stirred about. His whole body ached. He faced his head down and saw that his feet were reclined on a chair, while the rest of his body lay on the wet ground.

"I can't get up, it hurts," whined Brian.

"I should think it hurts. You just flew out of no where and hit the ground, nearly killing me in the process."

Brian shook his head. He could see that the figure was a female. She was around his age.

"I don't care what you tell me. I am dead! It was pouring rain out when I fell and the sky was dark grey."

"Okay, shut up. It just stopped raining a few minutes ago. The sun started shining too. I don't know where it came from."

"What in Christ's name were you doing out here in the rain."

"Enjoying it. I'd much rather bask in the rain than in the sun. I was sitting in a chair, rain- bathing."

"Who the fuck are you?"

"It doesn't matter. Get up. You're being a pussy," said the girl.

She reached her hand out and grabbed Brian's. She pulled Brian up very violently. He yelled loudly and she yelled back at him. Brian's upright stance lasted but a mere few seconds. He lost his balance and fell, hitting the girl. She fell also and he landed on top of her, with a face full of her dark hair. Before removing his face, he breathed in a very deep breath, and smiled as he breathed out.

"Your hair smells good," Brian said, crawling toward a chair.

"Well, I wash it."

Brian grabbed on to a chair and pulled himself up. When he was finally standing straight, he turned to the girl and looked her in the eyes. She was a thin, pale girl with long dark hair and braces. She was unattractive, but Brian didn't seem to notice. He just looked at her, not thinking at all.

"What?" she said.

"I'm Brian," he said, extending his hand. "What's your name?"

"Go fuck yourself," she said. She then smiled for the first time, and began to walk away.

Brian wasn't offended. He blushed, and combed his fingers through his damp hair. "You're mean!" Brian yelled out childishly. She didn't respond.

***

Brian limped to the elevator. As he went down, images of the girl's unattractive face ran through his mind, and the smell of her hair was stuck in his nose, and he couldn't get it out. He wasn't so sure that he found her attractive, but she was presently inhabiting his mind, and nostrils.

Brian limped to Mike's room. He knocked at the door. The red- haired girl answered.

"Where is everyone?" Brian asked.

She opened the door all the way, revealing everyone lying

in the beds and on the floors, some sleeping, others grinning, all reeking.

"Get in," she said. "I'm the only normal one."

Brian ignored her. He began to ramble to anyone who would listen.

"Yea well I'm confused. I hate my life, but I can't really remember why. I'm not so miserable. My back hurts really bad, though. Nearly died, you know. And now I want to go see the comedian. So get the fuck up all of you, because you're all my date."

CHAPTER 10

Brian awoke the next morning to shaking. He opened his eyes to find Melvin standing over him, moving him back and forth with his hands.

"Ah!" Brian screamed. "What the hell are you doing? You scared the shit out of me!"

"I'm waking you up. The boat's all docked and stuff. We get to go out today! We can shop and stuff!"

"Shop and stuff? Okay." Brian sat himself up in bed. "And how are you today?" he asked Melvin.

"Fine."

"Did you enjoy the comedy last night?"

"Yea, it was good, and how are you today."

"I don't know. I nearly died yesterday you know. The boat rocked and I fell over the rail and onto the pool deck. I woke up and all I saw was light, and then this dark figure came out of the light and made me get up. I thought it was God, but it was really just this girl with freckles."

"Freckles? Ha! Was she good looking?"

"I couldn't tell. She confused me. Her hair smelled really good though."

Brian stood up and yawned. Though he had been woken up by a force other than himself, he felt very well rested. He didn't want to go back to bed at all. He didn't know what he wanted, but he was sure that he wanted to be awake.

"I get first shower!" Melvin yelled, and ran into the bathroom, shutting the door behind him.

Melvin always took long showers, so Brian pulled on some pants, grabbed his room card, and went for a walk. He came to the hall where the stairs and elevators were. He decided that today seemed like a good day to live slowly, so he took the stairs. He walked at a steady, comfortable pace, unlike the day before when he ran up the stairs as fast as he could.

He walked across the pool deck, smiling. The sun was shining bright, not as bright as the heavenly sun of the day before, but bright. Brian ran his fingers through his hair, not as he had done so many times before, but with a god- like grace. He inhaled Mexico's air; the World's air, and a feeling came over him, a tingle if you will. For his life had nearly ended, but something had saved him. His life was still intact, now, for a reason. He believed the reason was that his life was meant to be lived, if it wasn't he would be dead right now. Life's passion that had died in Brian a few days earlier was miraculously rekindled. With the aid of the sun, the air, a tingle, and a freckly girl with braces, Brian was ready to give life one last try.

***

By the time Brian got back to his cabin, Melvin was out of the shower and dressed.

"Where were you?" Melvin asked.

"Just on the pool deck. It's really nice out, you know. I'm glad we docked today and not yesterday."

"Nice weather, that's good," Melvin said.

"Yea, I'm going to get in the shower now."

Brian took a quick shower, in which he shampooed his hair, washed his face and body, and brushed his teeth. When he got out of the shower, he put on shorts and a t- shirt. He quickly brushed his hair and then sprayed some cologne on his neck.

Brian and Melvin knocked at the cabin door of Edna and Harry.

"Good morning guys!" Harry exclaimed gleefully when he opened the door. "Are you all excited for today? I know that I sure am!"

"I am too!" yelled Edna from the room.

"I'm pretty excited," Brian said.

"Brian excited? Woo- hoo! Today's going to be a great day. Get your stuff, honey, and call the Parkers. Tell them we'll meet them at their room in a few minutes."

"They're coming?" Brian asked.

"They sure are. Why, is there something wrong?"

Brian gulped.

"Nothing wrong."

Brian had a frown on his face. He didn't want his good mood to be shot down. He wanted to live life happily. Then he realized that as passionate as he wanted to be toward life, he will always have problems. Brian couldn't run this time. He had to face Ashley. The old Brian would've sworn and thrown things. The new Brian, however, simply smiled a smile and accepted it.

Brian, Melvin, Edna, Harry, Tom, Jan, and Ashley all stood in line to get off the boat. Ashley clung to Brian and he felt uncomfortable. Melvin just stood there, looking at them, wishing that he was Brian. When they got off the boat, Brian was thrilled to see a familiar face. It was the face of none other than the vomit woman.

"Hey!" Brian yelled happily.

"Hello sweetie! I see you're all better!" said the vomit woman.

"I see you are too. So why are you just standing here all by yourself?"

"I'm waiting for my husband and my son. They're a bunch of dilly- dalliers."

"Honey, who is your friend?" asked Edna.

"This is..." Brian paused.

"I'm Betty," said the vomit woman, shaking Edna's hand. "Betty Kisnips."

"Betty Kisnips," Edna repeated. "Well it's nice to meet you, Betty. This is my husband, Harry. And these are our friends, Tom, Jan, and Ashley."

"And it's nice meeting you too. Oh look, there's the husband and son," said Betty, pointing to two people coming toward her. "It was nice seeing you all. Goodbye you two," she said to Brian and Melvin. "Hope you two keep your food in your stomachs for the rest of the cruise!"

"Bye Betty!" Brian and Melvin yelled simultaneously.

As Betty and her family walked away, a group of four made their way out of the ship. There was a large man with a beard who wore a Hawaiian shirt, a woman with large, gold framed sunglasses, a young man with short hair and a dirty look on his face, and a tall, thin girl with freckles and braces. It was the girl who had gotten Brian up after he fell.

"Hey!" Brian yelled to her.

She turned to him, gave him a dirty look, and continued walking with her family.

"Who was that?" Melvin asked.

"The girl who got me up when I fell over the rail."

Melvin chuckled.

"She's kind of ugly."

"Hmm."

"I know, she really is ugly, Brian," uttered Ashley. "You shouldn't talk to girls like her," she said, wrapping her arms around Brian.

***

The McMahons and the Parkers walked under the hot

Mexican sun. Edna and Jan were fanning themselves and complaining about how hot it was. Harry and Tom were busy talking about how glad they were, after walking by some poverty stricken Mexican people, to be Americans. Brian and Ashley walked side by side, against Brian's will of course. Ashley clung to him, giving him the occasional kiss on the cheek as they walked. Melvin just tagged along, envying Brian with all his heart.

Brian's temporary Siamese twin did not bother him in the least. In fact, he barely even payed attention to Ashley as she clung to him. His mind was racing and he had no chance to really pay attention to what was going on around him. All the walking he did was led by Ashley and all the talking he did was just a bunch of simple, one word answers.

The girl that Brian had fallen on had a family, like any normal person would. For some reason, seeing the girls family opened up a whole new world of thought for Brian.

So she has a family. Brian thought to himself, not knowing why he even cared.

"Look there," Melvin said, pointing. "That store looks cool. Let's all go in there."

"Sounds fine to me," said Harry with a grin.

The store was large. It had a roof, but no walls. There were flies buzzing all around. Upon entering, they were greeted by a chubby Mexican man who had ear rings and a ponytail.

"Hola," he said.

"Look honey, a real Mexican business man," said Edna, not realizing how dumb she sounded, to Harry.

"I know! Look at him. Isn't he great? Hello sir," Harry said, extending his hand to the Mexican man. "I'm Harry."

"Hola, Senor Harry. I'm Juan. Take a look in my store. We

have many nice things you can buy. Very good prices. Maybe you like some Tequila. We have the worm!"

"Yes. Thank you, Juan. We'll all take a look around."

They all spread out through the store. Harry and Edna went off to look at a bunch of coconuts that were painted to look like human heads. Tom and Jan went to look at the assortment of T-shirts. Melvin, naturally, went to look at the many pipes. There were pipes in every size shape and color.

"They're pretty," Brian said. "Melvin, you should buy some. I'm sure your going to be smoking some weed again before this is all over and done with. You might as well do it with something pretty."

"Yea, really pretty," Ashley said.

Juan snuck up behind them.

"Hola chicos! You guys like to smoke the weed? He he. These pipes, they very good for that. You want to buy?"

"I don't know. Maybe," Melvin said.

"Okay. Hey!" Juan said, looking at Ashley. "Hey mamacita! How you doin' ?"

He put his arm around her. "Hey mamacita!" he said again.

"Eew!" she yelled. "Brian! Get him off me!"

Juan let go. "Wow, mami. Just showin' a little love. No need to get all excited."

Brian didn't even hear Ashley's plea. His mind was somewhere else. The smell of the freckly girl's hair was still fresh in his nose, overpowering the thick smell of the Mexican shop. Though it was a good smell, Brian longed to smell something new, but was unable.

"Look here!" Melvin exclaimed, pointing to a shelf full of penis shaped whistles.

"Oh my God! They look like dicks!" Ashley exclaimed, smirking provocatively at Brian.

"Si. He he. When the chicas play the whistle, it looks like they suckin' the pee- pee," Juan said, pushing his tongue up against his cheek and laughing.

Edna overheard Juan's profane statement.

"Honey," Edna said, grabbing Harry's shirt. "I think we should leave. That Mexican man's acting all dirty and sexual. I don't want these kids hearing that sort of thing."

"Alright, sweetie. Let's go. Tom, Jan, we're going to head out. Are you guys coming?"

"Sure," Tom said.

They all left the store. The parents rambled on about how they thought Juan, and all Mexicans like him, were dirty men who thought about nothing but sex. Ashley was playing with Brian's hair as they walked. From time to time she would whisper in his ear, making comments about the penis whistle and his own penis, and giggling after. Melvin tried to talk to Brian a few times, and each time Brian tried to speak to him, but was interrupted by the attention starving Ashley. And on the very few occasions that Melvin tried to speak to Ashley, he was simply ignored.

They walked by a steaming stand with an elderly Mexican woman behind it. She was holding a crying baby.

"Burritos!" she screamed. "Real burritos! Yummy yummy! Only two American dollar!"

Brian lit up. He loved taco bell, so it seemed logical to him that he would like the real thing even more. He approached the stand with the yelling woman behind it, and inhaled. He expected the nice, beefy, spicy aroma of burrito to fill his nose, but all he smelled was the hair smell. Not since the brief moment when he was capable of smelling the world's air had he been able to smell anything other than the girls hair. He was annoyed. He wanted to experience the real burrito.

"Edna, buy me a burrito," Brian said, with Ashley still clinging to his arm.

"Oh no, honey. You don't want to eat food from there. Look how dirty that woman is. She's holding a baby. For all we know that little Mexican baby could've went pee- pee in the burritos. I'll buy you food somewhere else, somewhere that looks cleaner than this."

"Listen, Edna. I'm sure the little Mexican baby didn't go pee- pee in the God damned burrito," Brian said with a hint of sarcasm and a dash of bitchiness. "We're here because you want me to feel better. You want me to experience new things, right? If a real Mexican burrito from a real live dirty Mexican woman isn't a new thing in my life, I don't know what is. Buy me the friggen burrito right now!"

"Okay, okay. Don't make a scene," Edna said, blushing. "I didn't raise him to be so moody," she whispered to Jan.

The old Mexican woman handed Brian the burrito. The woman was ugly, but Brian ignored it. Somehow, ugliness became a part of life. It was no longer so strange.

Brian bit into the burrito. Beef and very hot sauce oozed out of it. Brian's taste buds did the macarena.

"Yum," Brian said slowly.

Edna and Harry smiled cheesy smiles.

"See, Edna. The Mexicans are good for something."

"Whatever makes you happy, honey."

Everyone in the group decided that they were hot and sweaty, and that they had seen enough for today. They were on their way back to the boat. While nearly everyone was busy thinking about how disgusting and dirty Mexico and its people were, Brian was thinking his own thoughts.

He thought this: Wow. So this is how it is in the rest of the world. The whole world isn't America. There are poor people who have to annoy rich Americans just to make a living. For some unfair reason, they were slapped down on earth and put into a shitty position. But they take what life's given them and they accept it. They do what they have to do. They eat what they have to eat. They fuck who they have to fuck. And why, because they have no choice, because that's where they ended up. Now look where I've ended up. Is it so bad? It's a pain, I get annoyed, but overall, is it so bad? Hm, I suddenly have the urge to do something I would never do. Maybe make an ass out of myself. Everything suddenly seems easy.

Brian's train of thought was interrupted by yelling.

"Senor Whiskers! Senor Whiskers! Would you like to buy some fresh mango?" yelled the voice of a Mexican man that Brian had yet to locate.

"Get the hell away from me, you smelly little man!" a deep voiced man yelled.

Brian, after a few moments of desperately spinning his head around, located the deep voiced man and the Mexican. The deep voiced man was the bearded man that Brian had seen earlier. He was with his family. The girl who Brian fell on was standing behind him.

"Listen, you stinky one! I didn't come here to be bothered by the likes of you! It's not my fault that you're poor. I came here to have a nice vacation with my family. So get the hell away from me."

The bearded man's family began to walk away. Brian chased after them. This was his chance to do what he felt like doing, making an ass out of himself.

"Wait!" Brian yelled.

The four members of the family all turned around at the same time. Brian jogged toward them. when he reached them he was huffing and puffing.

"We meet again," he said to the freckly girl who he had fallen on.

"What do you want. You keep acting like I wanted you to fall on me or something."

"You want me, don't you," he said, combing out his locks with his fingers. They were glistening in the sunlight.

"Hey you, leave my sister alone," intervened the mean-faced boy from earlier.

Brian ignored him.

"It's okay if you want me. Everyone does," Brian continued.

Edna, Harry, Jan, and Tom watched in disbelief. Ashley watched in anger. Melvin watched in confusion and disgust.

"Leave my fucking sister alone," repeated the mean-faced brother.

"Make me," Brian snapped.

The mean faced brother gave Brian a quick right fist to the nose. Brian fell to the ground and saw black.

***

Brian woke up in his bed in the cabin. Everyone he was with was standing over him, except for Ashley, who was sitting in his bed, rubbing his head. His whole head ached with excruciating pain. He began to breathe through his nose. He could smell Ashley's perfume and realized that the blow to his nose had given him his sense of smell back.

He moaned.

"Honey, what were you thinking?" asked Edna.

"I don't know," Brian said in a very nasally voice.

"Your nose could be broken, son," Harry said.

"Don't touch my nose! I want you all to leave. All of you but Melvin. Just get out I'm embarrassed."

"Are you sure that you're okay, honey?" Edna asked.

"Physically, yes. Mentally, I don't know. Now leave, all of you."

"Even me?" Ashley asked.

Brian grabbed her hand that she was using to rub his head and he squeezed it hard, looking her in the eye as he did so. She knew he wanted "even her" to leave.

As soon as they were gone, Brian turned to Melvin.

"What the fuck," Melvin said.

"I don't know what the fuck. She was intriguing."

"She's ugly though. You can have all these gorgeous girls, yet you want her. Do you even think she's good looking?"

"No, just interesting. And her hair smells good.

"That's what you want. An interesting girl with good smelling hair?"

"I don't know what I want."

"I will never understand you."

Melvin's emotions were battling each other. He wanted to kill Brian for being so confusing. Melvin wanted to slap him for making, what he thought, was a bad decision. Melvin wanted to hurt him just because Melvin wasn't him.

You're wasting what God gave you!" Melvin yelled.

"No, Melvin. It's so odd. You don't understand. I feel so, so, humanized. I feel like a real person lately. Suddenly my problems aren't so abnormal. Suddenly they're tolerable. Don't hate me, Melvin, I can't deal with it. You are my sanity. Now isn't tonight's dinner the formal one?"

Melvin sighed, still confused and angry.

"Yea, it is. why?"

"Good. Let's go get ready!"

"Why? Dinner's not for another four hours."

"Haven't you ever wanted to prance around in a suit for no good reason?" Brian asked, getting up out of his bed.

"You're fucking weird. No, I haven't."

"Well I have. Get dressed. It will be fun."

Brian and Melvin put their suits on. Brian sported a dapper, black pinstripe suit. With it, he wore a light blue shirt and a light blue and black, plaid tie. He had never looked more distinguished. Melvin threw on his beige suit, with a white shirt and a brown tie. He looked strange dressed this way.

"How do I look?" Melvin asked.

"Great," Brian said, covering his face to hide the smirk. "How do I look?"

"I love your blue shirt. It matches your nose."

Not bothered at all, Brian grinned.

***

Brian and Melvin ran around the ship like a bunch of nicely dressed five year olds. In one of the bars, they bumped into Betty Kisnips(the vomit woman).

"Betty, hi! How are you?" said Brian.

"Oh, hello dear. I'm fine. Wow, you look great. And you too," she said to both of them. "Dinner isn't til later, why are you already all dressed up?"

"Brian insisted. He's odd."

"I just felt like getting dressed up."

"Well there's nothing wrong with that."

"I have to go to the bathroom," Melvin said. "I'll be right back."

Brian stood talking to Betty for an hour before they both realized that Melvin had yet to return. Melvin is a big boy, they agreed, so they decided not to worry. Brian spoke to Betty another two hours. He told her all about his situation and how he came to have a blue nose. Betty was as confused as Melvin was. Betty, who was older than Brian's mother, was even a little hot for Brian. She didn't dare tell him that she was confused. He seemed happy, and she was the kind of person who liked to keep a happy person happy.

"Melvin's still gone. Dinner's in an hour. I should probably go see where he went. I'll definitely talk to you later though. Bye Betty!"

"Good bye! And good luck with that girl, for whatever reason you need luck!" Betty yelled, still extremely confused.

***

Brian went back to his cabin. He opened the door and saw Melvin sitting on his bed. His lap was covered with a blanket. On Brian's bed was an elephant made of towels.

"Look Melvin, Gerta made a towel elephant just like you wanted."

Melvin didn't reply.

"Where the hell have u been?"

Melvin's eyes were rolling back in his head and he was making face. The blanket that was coering his lap was moving. Brian, without giving it much thought, walked over and pulled the blanket away. Ashley parker was under the blanket and on her knees, with Melvin's private part in her mouth.

"Fuck! Jesus! Son of a Bitch! Goodbye!" Brian screamed, then stormed out of the room.

***

Brian, Edna, and Harry sat at their table, all dressed up and eating dinner in silence. Melvin never showed up at dinner, nor was in he the picture with the rest of the family.

After dinner, Brian went off by himself. He was walking on the third floor deck. He could smell the saltiness of the water. He could hear the waves . He looked over the rail and into the water, which was being tossed around by the boat, which was now on its way to it's next destination. After a moment of admiring the water and the again sniffable air, Brian continued walking. In the dark distance he could see someone looking over the rail, just as he had been doing moments before. As he grew closer, he saw that the person was the freckly girl with good smelling hair. He approached her with his head held high, well aware of the fact that she very well may throw him overboard.

"Hi," he said.

"Go away."

"Why?"

"I don't like you."

"You want me. I know it. It's okay if you do."

"You cocky piece of shit, you make me sick. Didn't my brother teach you to leave me alone?"

"He simply amused me."

"You're nuts."

Out of no where, the boat began to rock. The girl lost her balance and fell back. Brian fell on top of her.

There they were, lying face to face on the deck.

"You fucking bitch," Brian whispered softly.

She kissed him. He kissed her back.

CHAPTER 11

Brian returned to his room two hours later. Ashley was still there, but she and Melvin were sound asleep. Brian didn't care that Ashley was still there and he didn't care that he walked in on their sexual acts earlier.

Brian felt strangely lightheaded. He had spent the whole two hours on deck three with the girl, who's name, he found out, was Laurie Landersmith. During those two hours, they did not go farther than kissing each other. A feeling of Innocence came over Brian when he was in her presence. When he was with her, he felt no strong desire to do anything 'wrong'.

Brian was ready for bed. Gleefully, he kissed both Melvin and Ashley goodnight and tucked them in. He turned the lights off and crawled into bed. He was ready for tomorrow, which would be spent with Laurie.

***

Brian awoke the next morning feeling refreshed. He turned to Melvin's bed, and saw that Melvin was sleeping alone. He went and sat on the edge of the bed and began to shake Melvin's body.

Melvin's eyes opened.

"Huh. Hey, good morning," Melvin said, then yawned.

"I guess you got lucky last night."

"Yea, I guess I did."

"Where is she now?"

"We woke up real early. I walked her to her room. She didn't want to get into any trouble with her parents."

"So, are you happy now?"

"Well, you did have her first. But I kind of ignored that. Yes, yes I am happy now. We promised each other that we'd try to live. I feel, for once in my life, that I'm living the way I should be. I like sin, you know. It's always fun."

"I'm really happy for you, Melvin. But the good thing is, now I can be happy for me too."

"You can? Why is that?"

"I was with that girl all last night."

"The ugly one?"

Brian wasn't offended by the question. He knew the truth.

"Yes, the ugly one."

"I don't get you, man. I never will. But now that I'm getting some, I can't get angry at you. To each his own. You definitely have odd tastes though. Until now, I would consider you the exact definition of a perfectionist."

"I don't know. She seems so right. Something's there and it makes me happy, not like anything before. It's something though. And whatever it is, I think it's the reason I'm living for. I feel like I'm living life right too. Well, maybe not right, but I'm happy. I think in the long run, everyone's supposed to feel this feeling."

"I'm hardly going through a spiritual awakening like you seem to be, but I'm happy. I'm getting some, and that's what I wanted. And the best thing is, she lives right near us. Now I can get action whenever I want."

"Hm, I never asked Laurie where she was from. I was caught up in the moment. It didn't really occur to me. But anyways, how did the whole thing between you and Ashley even start?"

"Well," Melvin laughed. "I saw her walking in the halls. I said hi to her. For some reason she responded to be much differently than she usually does. She told me that she thought my suit was really cute and that beige was my color. The next thing I know, she's in the room blowing me."

"So, wow. Here we are. We're where we want to be. It's odd. As much as I wanted it, I didn't think it would happen," Brian said, slowly shaking his head.

"Me either."

"Yea. Well, I have to go get ready. I'm seeing her in a little while," Brian said, with more happiness than Melvin had ever seen him show.

Brian went into the bathroom to shower. Melvin sat on his bed, puzzled by Brian.

"I don't see the fuss about her," he whispered to himself.

Nonetheless, he was happy for Brian, as well as himself.

***

Brian and Laurie were pleasantly seated at a table on the pool deck. The sun was shining brightly. It complimented Brian's mood perfectly. He was sitting here, in the epitome of beautiful weather, with her. He felt so good that at times his situation seemed un- real. Though this all happened so abruptly, he did allow himself time to think. He was well aware of the fact that, by chasing after Laurie, he had contradicted himself to the point where the word contradiction seemed like an understatement. This contradiction, or whatever it was, was somewhat refreshing to Brian. This was part of his life, his new, flawed, human life that he intended to live to its fullest until its end.

"You make me feel like I've never felt before," Brian said to Laurie. "Even when I first saw you, after I fell off the deck, you made me feel something. I can't explain it, but now that I have it, I want to keep it."

"You give me a different feeling too, now that I've let you into my life."

"What kept you?"

"I've never had a boy in my life. No one's ever been interested in me. I'm underweight. I have braces to make my crooked teeth straight. I have a lot of freckles. On top of all that, I'm really moody, especially when it's that time of the month."

"That time of the month?" Brian said naively, for his inexperience with girls still shined through with a blinding light. "Never mind."

Brian was silent for a moment or two. To his dismay, he completely understood why she had never had a boy in her life. He knew she wasn't beautiful. He knew that her personality wasn't one that stood out among everyone else's in the world. There was something, though, some strange, incomprehensible force that drew him to her and made her flaws seem, in his eyes, completely right.

"You make me feel so, human."

"You make me feel pretty."

Brian remembered a movie he once watched with Edna, a Lifetime original. He hated Lifetime and all of its movies and T. V. shows, but on one occasion, a line from a movie really touched Brian and made him think. It was a film about a lesbian love affair, a very unconventional and sometimes misunderstood thing. Defending her relationship with another woman, the main character of the movie said this, "When you truly fall in love with some one, they are perfect. Not because people are perfect. I assure, no person in the world is perfect. It's because, when you truly fall in love with someone, their flaws become meaningless to you. She has flaws, but I love them. And I love her!"

Laurie was clearly a flawed girl, which made Brian think this: It can't be. Or maybe it can. It's love! I'm in love!

"I think I love you," Brian blurted out quickly.

Laurie paused.

"I'm pretty sure I love you too," she said.

"Love, I like love." Brian laughed the laugh of a boy in love. "So, tomorrow we'll be docking in Progreso. Then the day after tomorrow we'll be at sea all day. And the next morning we'll be arriving back in New Orleans. Two more days. We have two more days."

"Why do you sound so unhappy. The cruise has two more days, not us. We have lives outside of this boat, not that I miss mine. Who's to say you can't be part of my life once this little trip is all over? And who's to say that I can't be a part of yours?"

"No one's to say anything!" Brian yelled. "I don't even know where you live!"

"Well, I live in Louisiana. That's where the boat left from. Even if you live in a different part of the state, we can still see each other."

Brian swore, then began slapping himself in the face.

"What's wrong?"

"I don't live in the same state as you. I live in Boston. We had to take two planes just to get into New Orleans to get on the boat."

"No."

"Yes."

"No.

"You don't understand, yes."

Laurie began to sob.

"Don't cry. We'll figure something out. I promise."

She stood up from the table.

"I, I, I have to go," she said. "I'll see you later."

She leaned toward his face to kiss him. Then, only inches away, she pulled back. Then she ran.

Brian, head in his hands, then began to cry himself. His desire to live life to it's fullest suddenly seemed to be slipping away.

***

Brian knocked at the door of Mike's cabin.

"Brian, what's up?"

"Do you have anything that can make me unable to think?"

"Sure thing, man. Come on in."

***

Brian banged at the door of his cabin, for his vision was far too impaired for him to be able to fit the key card into its slot.

Melvin opened the door.

"Brian, what's up? You look upset."

"Yea, uh," Brian said. His speech was slurred. "I took some pills and drank some stuff. I hope I'm not interrupting anything," he said, seeing Ashley sitting on Melvin's bed.

"Well, you kind of are. But that's okay. Come in."

"Okay."

Brian stumbled into the room, then fell onto his bed.

"Why are you like this? What happened?" Melvin asked, concerned.

Brian sighed, then wiped sweat from his forehead. His face was covered with sweat and his clothing was stained with it.

"She lives in Louisiana! After this, I will never see her again! I went to Mike's room after and he gave me some stuff. It made me like this. I really don't feel any better. I just can't stand straight. Speaking clear is hard too."

"Who is he talking about?" Ashley asked.

"That girl he made a fuss over, remember?" Melvin said

"Oh, the ugly one?"

Brian let out an animal- like shriek, then began to bawl his eyes out.

"It's okay, really," Melvin said, putting his arm around Brian. "It just wasn't meant to be."

"But it was! It was meant to be. I fell from the sky right onto her and then the light was shining! It was meant to be! Nothing has ever been meant to be more than this!"

"Eh, I'm sorry," Ashley said, running over to Brian. She began to stroke his head.

"Maybe we can make you feel better," Melvin said.

Brian leaned over, then puked on the floor.

"Ashley, go wet some towels and knock at my aunt an uncle's door. Ask them for some Nyquil. I'll sing to him."

Brian was crying, now, worse than he was before. He reeked of puke.

"Brian! Ignore the shit you're in! Cuz Brian, you have such nice, even skin! Brian! You make girls happy everywhere! And Brian, you have such pretty colored hair! Brian! No matter where you go! Oh, Brian! You know we'll always love you so!"

"Stop it! Stop!" Brian screamed, then he puked.

Ashley returned.

"Here I am! I have the Nyquil and some wet cloths. Here they are," she said.

Melvin took a wet face cloth, folded it, and placed it on Brian's forehead.

"How does that feel?"

"Wet!"

"Here, take some of this," Melvin said, putting the whole bottle of Nyquil to Brian's mouth.

Brian took a swig.

"That'll make you feel better!" Ashley said, jumping. Her breasts bounced.

Brian leaned back. He began to breathe easily. Though he was still crying very hard, he was looking at Melvin and Ashley, who were sitting next to each other on Melvin's bed. He was smiling at him. They were smiling back. When Brian's smile grew to an all time wide, his eyes began to roll back into his head.

He started to speak.

"Great! Great you guys. I love you guys so much. Remember that time in the food store. I shit myself. You wiped my bum, Ashley. I'll never forget that. And fucking mother ish me go to the.." Brian was asleep.

Melvin and Ashley stared at the sleeping Brian for five straight minutes without speaking. Ashley broke the silence.

"He looks dead."

"He looks peaceful.

"You think he'll wake up any time soon?"

"Probably not."

She jumped on him and proceeded to tear his shirt off.

***

Three hours later, Brian, who was in a coma- like slumber, sprung up out of no where.

"Ah!" he screamed. Melvin and Ashley scrambled to put their clothes on.

"I had a dream! They said if I stay here, my life will be over! I have to fix things, right now!"

Brian started for the door, ran into it, fell on his back, stood up, brushed his ass off, and turned to Ashley and Melvin.

"Oops," he said, then opened the door and left.

***

Brian banged at Laurie's can door like a man possessed. Her brother answered.

"Laurie, where is she."

"You can't see her."

Brian kicked him in the crotch and he fell over. Brian entered the cabin. Laurie was lying on one of the beds, still crying. Brian threw himself on her.

"We can't do this. We can't be stupid. We have two days left and I refuse to waste them."

"Okay."

With no intentions of letting go any time soon, he embraced her.

CHAPTER 12

Your eyes match your nose," Melvin said to Brian. It was the next morning. They had both just gotten out of bed.

"Yea, well her brother wouldn't let me in their room to see her. I kicked him in the nuts. When he got up, he pulled me off of her, and knocked me out again."

"That sucks."

"Yea. The abuse you take for love."

"Love, really?"

"I'm almost positive."

"Wow."

"Yea. So Melvin, this is the first time we've been alone in a while. I've missed you the past few days. I mean, I've been around you enough. But I miss just you, you know, talking and stuff. I can't talk to just anyone about this stuff. It's kind of funny. I always feel like you're jealous of me. I never really understood why. The girls always flocking around me was never fun. I didn't like any of them. Nothing was there. Now that I've finally found something, something good, it's being taken away. For the first time, no offence, I can honestly say that I'm jealous of you."

"Why the hell are you jealous of me? I have what I want, a hot girl to release my sexual frustrations on. There's no substance. But hey, I'm not a substance kind of guy. I'm happy. You couldn't be happy this way. In the long run, you're the lucky one. You're the one who'll care in the end, who'll protect her in the end, who'll provide for her in the end. You're best at loving and I'm best at lusting. You have no reason to be jealous of me."

"But I'm unhappy," Brian said, slapping his thighs.

"You're allowed to be unhappy though! What's happened to you isn't fair. You've been handed a good thing and now it's being ripped away and there's nothing you can do about it!"

"Don't rub it in."

"I wasn't finished. Brian, you used to always ramble on about getting what you want. And I did too. I got what I wanted. I always knew what I wanted. You got what you wanted, and it was nothing like how either of us expected it to be. We both expected you to want perfection, but instead you wanted Laurie!" Brian snarled. "No, no, no, listen! You got what you wanted, that's all that needs to be said. And now it's being taken away. It's how life works. I know that it's easier to say than experience, but you've been thinking a lot about life lately, I know. You understand how life works a hell of a lot better than I do. Don't just ignore what you understand so well. You know that life is unfair and I think that you've pretty much accepted life. This is the bad side of life, Brian. You'll see good times again, I know you will. But the only way you can see them is if you get through with this. You've been strong lately. Don't turn weak on me. If you go insane, what will that say about me. I am your sanity after all. Come on, don't make me look bad."

Over the past few days, Brian had been so busy with trying to find happiness. During that period of time, he had forgotten exactly why Melvin was so important to him. Now, after that lecture, he remembered. It was lectures like that that got Brian through life. Brian and Melvin fed off of each other's experience since they could remember. When one of them lacked something, they always looked for it in the other. Right now, Brian lacked a great deal, and Melvin was there for him, ready feed him all that he lacked.

"I'll do my best to stay sane. I promise that if I decide to become irrational, I'll ponder it first."

There was a knock at the door.

"Who's that?" Brian asked.

"It's Ashley."

"Why?"

"We docked this morning. We're going shopping together."

Melvin opened the door.

"Hello!" Ashley exclaimed as she entered.

"Hey," Melvin said. He kissed her on the lips.

"Well don't mind me. I'm sure you guys might like a nice quickie before shopping." Brian laughed. Melvin cackled. Ashley blushed. "I'll see you guys later!"

Brian hugged them both, then left.

***

Like Melvin and Ashley, Brian and Laurie left the boat to shop. As they walked the dirt streets, they were completely exposed to the sun. They were covered in sweat and after a half hour of walking, they were already sun burned.

The walked by a fish market. The thick smell of decaying fish was unavoidable. Brian and Laurie both wanted to puke. Just as they passed the fish market, Melvin and Ashley passed the other way. They were holding each others' hand and they were both smiling. Brian looked at Laurie. Her unattractive face glowed with the kind of beauty that the most beautiful women envy. There was something in the air alright, something other than the odor of rotting fish, that is. And that something certainly seemed like love.

"Look at them," Brian said, pointing to Melvin and Ashley. "That makes me happy. Look at Melvin's face. Seeing him like that makes me feel good. Being with you makes me feel so good. It's feelings like these, they're the real pleasures in life. You can't buy feelings like these."

"No, you can't," Laurie said.

"I promised Melvin that I'd stay sane through all of this, Laurie. You have to help me stay sane. You have to be stern. If I show any signs of losing it, take immediate action. You have the biggest effect on me. Love has the biggest effect on me."

"I won't let you go insane."

"Good. And tomorrow, we have to spend the whole day together. Promise we can spend the whole day together."

"I promise."

"We'll make sure that we never forget tomorrow."

Tears began to form in both of their eyes.

"Never forget."

"We can do all sorts of fun things. Then we can get all dressed up and have a nice, romantic dinner. And then..." he began to cry. "Jesus Christ! There's so much fucking shit I want to do and so little time to do it. God damn it! Fuck!"

Laurie started to cry, much harder than Brian was.

"Stop it! Be realistic. We can't live our whole lives out tomorrow. Sanity, I have to be stern." the tears began to flow at an all time maximum. "But being stern with you is so fucking hard. Your black eye and your blue nose, they're so fucking cute."

There they stood, in the middle of a smelly, Mexican street, with only their anticipation for the next day to keep them from breaking down.

CHAPTER 13

This is going to be the most loving day, Melvin," Brian said.

It was the next day now. Melvin had just woken up, but Brian was awake the whole night, pondering exactly what he and Laurie would do this day.

"The most loving day? Well I'm glad you're being so positive about this all. Maybe keeping your sanity won't be so hard after all."

"I don't think it will. I did all my mourning and crying yesterday. I think, after all that, I have a good head on my shoulders now."

"That's good."

"It is. What are you going to be doing today?"

"Something with Ashley."

"You don't know what?"

"No, not yet."

"Hmm. I'm getting in the shower."

"Okay."

Brian spent forty- five minutes in the shower. He wanted everything about this day to be clean, and nice, and refreshing. Even his armpits.

When he gout out of the shower, there was a knocking at the door. It was Edna.

"Yes?"

"Hi honey!"

"Hi, Edna."

"Oh come on, call me mom."

"No. What do you want?"

"It's our last day here. We should all do something as a family."

"No."

"That wasn't a question."

"You say that as if you think I'm a considerate person who cares."

"Honey, we're going to spend the day as a family whether you like it or not."

All the blood in Brian's body ran to his head, but his head was far too small to hold all of his body's blood. His face was redder than anything "that time of the month" could produce. Something inside of him snapped.

"No! We are not spending the day as a family! I don't care! I don't fucking care!" he screamed, adding extra emphasis to the word fucking. "There are things that need to be done today. Not things I want to do, but things I need to do. I fucking need to. You are not stopping me. I will eat your fucking face off, Edna. You are so fucking perky. God damn you. Ahhhh!"

She slapped him in the face.

"You're fucking nuts," she said.

Brian was speechless. Edna slammed the door and left.

"Sanity, Brian. Don't make me look bad," Melvin said sternly.

"Today is going to be the most loving day," Brian said again. He walked to his suitcase, reached into a compartment in it, and pulled out a very large wad of cash. "Now I'm off to see her."

Brian breathed a deep breath and smiled. Then he left.

***

Brian knocked at Laurie's cabin door. Her brother answered. Brian looked him dead in the eye.

"Laurie," he said coldly.

"No," said her brother.

"I'll hurt you," said Brian, with a dangerous look in his eye.

"I'll kill you."

"You'll be in too much pain to kill anyone, you rotting, disgusting, fucking cunt."

Her brother moved away from the door.

"She's in here."

Brian patted him on the head and smiled.

"Thank you," he said, laughing. The brother blushed. "Don't you look pretty," Brian said when he saw Laurie.

"Thank you. You look quite pretty yourself."

He took her hand.

"Shall we?"

"Yes."

***

Brian led her to an elevator. When they got on, he pressed the second floor button. She asked him where they were going, but he refused to tell. "It's a surprise," he told her. "I promise that you'll like it."

They got off on the second floor.

"There's nothing on this floor. What are we doing here."

"There's gift shops."

"So..."

"Come on."

He brought her to a jewelry store in the gift shop hall.

"What are we doing here?"

"What do you want?"

"What do you mean?"

"I have a very large wad of cash in my pocket, Laurie. I can't let you go without anything to remember me by. It'd be nice if the thing you have to remember me is a particularly expensive thing. I don't want you to pick up some plastic key chain and say, 'Ah. I miss Brian.'"

"Are you sure?"

I love her, of course I'm sure, Brian thought.

"Yes, I'm very sure."

***

So they walked back to the elevator. Laurie had a new, sparkly ring on her finger. Brian still had some of the large wad of cash left.

"Today's going to be such a good day," Brian said.

"It's already off to a good start."

And what a good start it was. She had been swooned and blinded by Brian's act. Brian knew that he had swooned her. The girl Brian was so sure he loved was now a walking blob of glowing affection.

Brian touched her nose because it was so darn cute. She smiled at him and her braces sparkled like her ring.

***

The elevator reached the ninth floor, the pool deck. They went to the buffet room and they both got a large lunch, which they brought out to the pool deck.

"Isn't this great," Brian said. "Look how nice the sun is today. It's so warm too. I think people take the sun for granted some times. It's always there, but does anyone really ever stop to admire its beauty?"

"You do."

"Do you?"

"Well not until now. But now that you said it, it is really beautiful. It's just so big and colorful. It makes days like today even better. Anything that can do that must be great."

"You're like the sun, Laurie. I think people take you for granted. You're always there, and you're always beautiful. But no one realizes it, not until it's pointed out anyway. Once people stop to admire you, they'd be in awe, I swear. I think I can see real beauty. I appreciate things that need to be appreciated. My ability to do that makes me feel really good."

Brian was sure, now, that he had life all figured out. He was only seventeen, but what he was experiencing right now was real life and real love. He was sure of it. After this one week of a search for something greater, that greater something had been found. And now that it had been found, there was no other way. As far as Brian was concerned, there was nothing else on the world that existed that could make him feel the way he was now. This was the way his life was meant to be! How could anything else make sense at this point?

**

After lunch, they went up onto the top deck. There, they spent three hours playing shuffle board. They cracked foolish jokes, embraced each other every here and there, and felt happy. Their hair blew in the wind. It was the perfect stereotype for a scene out of a romantic comedy film.

It was five o' clock now. They were lying on reclining deck chairs, drinking tropical drinks. Their conversation was practically non- existent. For they had discussed everything there was to discuss. They shared no friends, no common interests, just an incomprehensible longing desire to be with each other.

Brian turned to her and saw that she was already looking at him.

"Yes?"

"You're gorgeous," she said.

"Thank you. So are you."

"No! It's not that way. You're un- real. Like a dream. That's how gorgeous you are."

"Dinner's soon, sweetie. Maybe we should go get ready?"

"We have close to two hours."

"Today has been so great so far. So much love that it's overwhelming. I feel like I might pass out from ecstasy. Plus, I might take a while to get ready. I want to look perfect for you. I want us to remember tonight," Brian said in a strangely casual manner.

She pushed her chair over so that she was sitting right next to him. She leaned her head on his shoulder and giggled like the mass of perky, feminine affection that she was.

"You can't look any better than you do!" she said, excited.

"I bet you I can," Brian said. "So, shall I escort you to your room to get ready?"

"Fine."

Brian walked Laurie to her room. As he walked away, he began to mumble to himself.

"Today was such a loving day, and it's just going to get better," he said, with what seemed like self- doubt. "And I love her. I love her. I love her," he repeated again and again like a broken record.

***

Brian sported a well fitting, neatly cut, three buttoned grey suit. He wore it with a straight collared white dress shirt and a black tie with diagonal white stripes. He, for the first time in a long time, put gel in his hair. He belonged on the wall of every teenage girl in America.

Laurie was in a short, pink, sleeveless dress. She had her hair down and straight. She belonged on the wall of no where, except maybe the living room in her home.

"You look stunning," Brian said when he saw her.

"You look..." she was speechless.

She wanted his ass.

***

It was dark now. Brian and Laurie sat at a lone table on the pool deck, ready to eat buffet food. They had brought the food to a table on the pool deck because it was quieter out there and because, Brian thought, eating dinner under the moonlight would be much more romantic than eating dinner in a room with a bunch of loud families.

"How's the chicken?" Brian asked.

"It's good."

"That's good. Yea, uh, look at me. I'm fucking ridiculous. I have so much on my mind that I'm talking about chicken. We aren't here to talk about chicken. I am in denial. Who the fuck are we fooling? Are we ever going to see each other again? We're sitting here like everything's fine."

"Don't talk that way," Laurie said, with seriousness that one of her age should be unable to express.

"I know it's bad. But every time we try to have fun, the conversation always gets back onto these bad subjects."

"Don't get mad at me, Brian. You're always the one who brings all this stuff up. It's never me who does it."

"I'm so confused. I've been lost for so long. I didn't know what I was going to do with myself. Then you came along, turned my life upside down. What I needed in my life, you've given me. Now, what I need is being snatched away. I don't think I deserve this and I can hardly handle it! You have to understand!" Brian said, as sincerely as he could sound.

"Of course I understand, I just don't want to think about it. You're so gorgeous."

"Don't say that. I think we should call it a night. The chicken suddenly looks so unappetizing. I'll walk you to your room. Come on."

There was silence in the elevator. Brian and Laurie didn't speak or look at each other. Brian was in the middle of a serious mental battle with himself. He was assuring himself that he loved her. He didn't know why it was so important to convince himself that he loved her, he should already be sure of it. But he couldn't help but doubt himself. It just seemed like the right thing to do.

The two under- aged victims of each other's presence stepped out of the elevator. Brian was still busy fighting with himself, and Laurie was holding back tears.

They came to Laurie's cabin.

"Brian, why don't you come in. I don't want to say goodbye this way."

"This is a bad situation. If I come in there, it won't make it any better."

"Make love to me," Laurie said, trying to sound like a woman.

"What?"

"You heard me. Make love to me. Let's end this with something to really remember."

Brian stepped back. This was the first time that the idea of sex had ever entered his mind when it came to Laurie. To put it bluntly, Brian did not want to have sex with her now, nor did he ever. His desire to be with her came from something other than that.

What makes you want to be with me?"

"I love you."

"What drives you to love me?"

"You're just so, so.."

"Gorgeous? I can't have sex with you. I don't want to have sex with you. I don't want to ruin the innocence that I thought we had. I thought this was innocence. I thought we had something like no one else in the world had. Is everything sex? Yea. This is the way life is, isn't it? Goodnight, Laurie."

Brian moved in close to her, as if he was going to kiss her. She puckered her lips to receive their final kiss. But he grabbed a handful of her hair, put it to his nose, and inhaled.

"What a nice smell," Brian said, then walked away.

CHAPTER 14

It was the next morning. Brian and Melvin had just finished getting all of their things together.

The cruise was over. They had docked in New Orleans during the night. In a matter of hours, they would be on a plane home.

They said their good byes. They spent a few minutes with Betty Kisnips. They thanked Gerta for keeping their room clean. They thanked Mike for getting them high all those times. They were ready to go.

***

"I was thinking about being irrational, like I said. I really pondered. I decided not to be though," Brian said to Melvin. They were sitting on the plane.

"You shouldn't have been irrational. She wasn't worth it."

"She wanted to have sex with me."

"And you said no?"

"Yes."

"I would have too. But you obviously looked at her in a much different way than I did. Why did you say no?"

"I don't know, I just didn't want to I guess."

"I knew you couldn't have really wanted her that way Brian. I know you so well. Not to sound like a prick, but you were lost and confused. You didn't know what to do."

"I'm lost! Look at you," Brian yelled. Edna turned around and told him to be quiet.

"I knew exactly what I wanted. I found it, and I was happy. You were never too sure, Brian. You knew you could have any girl in the world. I think life got boring to you. I think you just wanted someone to talk to. Relationships aren't all about talking!"

"I can't reply to that," Brian said quietly. "Leave me alone. I want to take a nap."

EPILOGUE

Brian took a seat on the crowded train. It felt surprisingly good to ride a train into the city once again. Brian looked at the people around him. Sitting directly across from him was an elderly black man. He and Brian locked eyes. Brian smiled and winked his eye at him. The elderly man nodded his head and waved.

Brian was on his way to the doctor's office. Hubbard requested that she have a meeting with Brian immediately after he returned from the vacation.

***

"The doctor will see you now," said the woman behind the desk, only moments after Brian had made himself comfortable.

Brian entered Hubbard's office with his head held slightly higher than usual.

"Hello, doctor," he said with an odd grin. "How are you?"

"Very well, Brian. And how are you?" Hubbard asked, patting her immensely large stomach.

"Different."

"Different? Hmm. Different in a good way or different in a bad way?"

"I'm not too sure."

"Well let's find out. Why don't you have a seat, and we

can try to figure out what exactly has changed since the last time we met."

For the first time, Brian did not dread spilling his guts to the doctor. He would have gladly rambled on for hours about exactly how he felt. The only problem was that he didn't know how he felt. He knew that he had gone through a huge change. Some how, nothing felt the same, but he had no idea where the changes in him even were.

"So, how was your little cruise?" asked Hubbard in her deep, chubby voice.

"A lot happened."

"A lot happened? Well, why don't you tell me about the a lot of stuff that happened."

"I, I don't know."

"Did you meet a girl?"

"A few?"

"You were a ladies man on the boat? I can't say that really surprises me. You're a very good looking young man. You're charming too, in your own unique way. But you say 'a few' so reluctantly. And I find it sort of odd that you say a few. You always seemed so dead set on spending the rest of your life with just one girl. I mean, you haven't touched a girl in your entire life just because you didn't want to waste your effort on the wrong one. Now you tell me that in the period of a week you were involved with more than one girl. It sounds kind of odd to me, Brian. Why don't you explain what went on?"

"Okay. One night, I was feeling a little uh, discombobulated. I was wandering aimlessly. The next thing I know, I'm waking up the next morning and I'm in bed, naked, with some girl I've never seen in my life. She's real pretty though. I don't even mean pretty. She's beautiful. I was so excited. I thought that she would be the one. I mean, I lost my virginity to her. Even tho I didn't remember it, she had to be the one. You know how I am, no matter what state I'm in I wouldn't lose my virginity to just anyone."

"Go on."

"So, it turns out that my parents know her parents, and that the whole family lives in Boston. I'm thinking, wow this is great. I was sure that she was the one. It just seemed so, meant to be. But then I finally got the chance to meet her when I was in the right frame of mind. She wasn't what I expected. She was all wrong. I mean, she made me feel so happy. She just wasn't it. I can't explain it," Brian said, then stopped talking.

"Is that it? You said that there was more than one."

"There were two girls I had something to do with."

"Well why don't you tell me about the other one."

"That subject is kind of touchy. She's the one that really changed the way I feel."

"You lost your virginity to the first girl, yet the subject of the second girl is more difficult to talk about? I don't understand."

"I fell in love."

"Are you sure?"

"It felt like it."

"What happened?"

"Well. There was a storm. The boat was rocking and I fell over the top deck and blacked out. When I woke up, this girl was standing over me. She wasn't so great looking. But there was something there that made me pursue her, this weird feeling I never felt before in my life. I mean, you get these weird tingly feelings when you're attracted to someone, but this wasn't it. This was something greater than a tingle, something you don't feel very often.

"So anyways, I went after her, and she didn't seem

interested. I was kind of surprised. I kept on trying, and eventually, after a lot of work, we got involved with each other. My God, it was the best thing ever. I could sit around for hours with her, just talking. She was so much fun. When I was with her, there weren't any hormones interrupting my relationship with her. It felt so innocent and it made me feel like a good person. Then, when everything seemed so great, I found out that she lives half way across the country. I, of course, was crushed. So, on the last day of the cruise, I tried to spend a great, loving day with her. Everything seemed to be going fine. Then, suddenly, angry emotions started flowing out of me. After that, she asked me to have sex with her. I said no and left. I didn't see her again."

"Wow, very dramatic," Hubbard said in a serious tone of voice. "But, you don't know why you liked her so much?"

"I told you, I can't explain it."

"Did you find her very physically attractive?"

"My attraction to her had nothing to do with anything physical."

"Hmm. I think maybe you just needed somebody to talk to."

Brian stood up. He stomped his foot on the ground.

"No! No! Why would I do that? I bought her a big expensive ring. Why would I buy her a big expensive ring just because I liked talking to her?"

"You said yourself that you couldn't explain how you felt. Unexplainable actions go hand in hand with unexplainable feelings, Brian. I think that you might've been confused."

"I don't know."

"Brian, you have to understand that the whole trick behind living life as a human being is to realize that life isn't perfect. You're just like everyone else, Brian. I just think that you haven't realized it yet. Everyone realizes it. It's only a matter of time before you do too. I think this session is over," Hubbard said rudely. She caressed her fourth chin. "You can leave now."

***

Brian got on the train to go home. After the meeting with Hubbard, he felt even more lost than he had before

His lost feeling was blocked out when he spotted a blonde, about his age, sitting a few seats away. He got up and walked toward her. She looked up at him and giggled. He sat next to her.

"Hi," he said.

"Hi."

Brian felt a tingle in his chest.

***

One week later, Brian sat down at his computer to type. This is what he typed:

Dear Laurie,

Hi, it's Brian. I felt that sending you this letter would be the right thing to do. After meeting you, everything about me has changed. It's odd. Life isn't the same. Suddenly I have my whole life ahead of me, something that I've never realized before. Somehow you've helped me figure this out. You are an important person in my life and you always will be. I want to thank you for helping me the way you did.

Well, I met someone. She's blonde. Her name's Molly. She's pretty nice I guess. She's pretty normal. When I'm with her, I feel normal too. It's kind of good. This doesn't erase you from my mind, though. Memories of you will always be there somewhere, I'm sure. You were great to talk to. And you will always have the best hair I've ever smelled.

Sincerely,
Brian.

***

Later that day, Brian mailed his typed up letter. He thought about Laurie once, and only once. He smirked, combed his fingers through his hair, and walked away into the rest of his life.

The End